# Switching to ON!

## The 2025 SebArts Writers Anthology

Editors:
Susan E. Gunter
Linda Loveland Reid

Assistant Editor:
Corinne Asturias

Switching to ON!
The 2025 SebArts Writers Anthology

Front cover art: Kim Winter
Back cover art: Brian R. Martens
Book design: Jo-Anne Rosen

ISBN: 978-1-941066-71-3

Wordrunner Press
Petaluma, California

It is our pleasure to dedicate this anthology to Sebastopol Center for the Arts. It is through their programming that we have come together to explore and hone our craft.

SebArts is the cultural hub of Sonoma County, offering a huge array of opportunities, including open studio programs (Art Trails and Art at the Source), a ceramic studio, film festival, art gallery exhibits, poetry and writer workshops, art classes, emerging artist program, and even a chorus. For this, and much more, we thank you.

# Contents

# Introduction to *Switching to ON!* The 2025 SebArts Writers Anthology

At Sebastopol Center for the Arts, community is at the heart of everything we do—and nowhere is that more beautifully expressed than in our Writers Salon. This anthology is more than a collection of poems, stories, and reflections. It is a testament to the creative power that emerges when people come together to write, listen, and grow in community.

The SebArts Writers Salon has become a gathering place for writers of all backgrounds and levels of experience. Each month, participants share new work, offer thoughtful feedback, and engage in conversations that build trust, vulnerability, and inspiration. Together, they've created something rare and essential: a space where stories are nurtured and voices are honored.

Poetry and prose born from this kind of community carry something extra—they carry witness. They remind us that storytelling is not a solitary act, but one deeply rooted in relationship. In a time when many writers face isolation, censorship, or creative burnout, the ability to write together in support and solidarity is more important than ever.

At SebArts, we believe that literary arts are vital to cultural life. They help us imagine new futures, confront difficult truths, and celebrate what connects us. The pieces in this anthology reflect the strength, depth, and joy of a local writing community committed to those ideals.

We are honored to share this collection with you. It represents the spirit of SebArts: creative, collaborative, courageous.

Thank you to all the writers, facilitators, and readers who make this work possible—and to you, for opening these pages and joining the conversation.

Serafina Palandech
*Executive Director*
707.829.4797 x1007

## Editors' Notes

Crazy-weird, exciting, and emotional are all words to describe our writing adventures together. When we started this salon two years ago, there were no expectations. What happened is amazing.

Our writers are experimental and traditional. Their prose and poetry fill our minds with mystery and wonder. And did I say, excellent writing! It's been an honor to be part of this effort.

Thank you, Sebastopol Center for the Arts, for sponsoring our group. We are grateful, excited, and proud.

— Linda Loveland Reid, Co-Facilitator and Editor

I was excited when Linda asked for a volunteer to help her teach the Writers' Salon, though I wasn't sure what to expect: I have been overwhelmed by the talent in our group. Writing styles and subjects vary widely, something that allows each participant to gain new perspectives. The critiques that each writer offers others have been probing and helpful. We respect one another's work, giving all of us space to grow. I am grateful to the Sebastopol Center for the Arts for sponsoring this group.

— Susan E. Gunter, Co-Facilitator and Editor

# Corinne Asturias

Corinne Asturias is a former journalist, college instructor, columnist and cultural anthropologist living in Sebastopol. She has written about many subjects including politics, the environment and inspiring people which led her to interview the late and legendary Mister Fred Rogers and *Wild* author Cheryl Strayed. These days she is fascinated by the interconnectedness of humans, the animal kingdom and the natural world; she writes poetry, nonfiction and fiction.

Corinne served as Features Editor for *The Press Democrat*, where she managed six sections and was part of the newsroom that received the Pulitzer Prize in 2018.

# Fickle Bounty

*Corinne Asturias*

Today I meander through the apple trees
In the way, way back of my yard
Devoid of fences and human yearnings
Among living statuary I call friends
Skeletal survivors of an orchard planted long ago,
Before I lived here, before notions of yield ran the soil ragged
Before precision and perfection ruled

Somehow, it still works, this scramble of bending boughs
Black goblins hunched against a gold shag carpet —
Weighted with apples this time of year: green with red
    streaks
Or red with green, some striped lipstick pink
And in the tall grass sleep the tawnies:
Overripened, sun-stroked yellow with crimson
Whispering sweetness from the sun

Worms live in some, pushing their scat out the door,
Bruises, wild turkey bitemarks and piles from deer
Remind me this harvest is a shared one; I mustn't be greedy.
Bird pecks, bee licks, bruises from the falls, night dirt
Yet every ten apples or so, somehow, a still-perfect specimen
Rests on soft grass to be eaten whole, like the ones
My mother used to put in my lunch

Unlike the groomed trees in the front yard
These confide what nature does every year,
Without sprinklers and loppers and clay pots
Leaching the liquor of fortified soil into the earth
Sentinels of winter nights and gnawing winds,
Searing days and misty mornings
These trees stand sturdy and scraggly as owls

Some would call this orchard neglected, dying
A vestige of a vanished time and
Desiccated dreams, farm dynasties and fields
Gone to seed, never to return
Yet I savor it here, amid the fickle bounty
Studying the echoes of imperfection
Knowing their truths are sound

# Reapers

*Corinne Asturias*

Some of my best friends are vultures
That gouge and rip upon the flesh
Of roadkill and those less fortunate
And relish doing so, somewhat noisily,
Bragging loudly about it after the fact.

You've seen them circling unapologetically
After the worst of storms and calamities,
Calculating opportunists who
Inquire with minute tilts and glances:
Anybody not feeling so great? Anybody dead?

And why have they gotten such a bad name,
These humble cleaners who mop up misfortune
Flying with the precision of pilots in formation?
Their taut underwings trimmed in chocolate,
They remind us: perspective is everything

I chanced upon a fallen one last winter
Splayed on the grass below power lines after a storm
Its ebony wings in the shape of a cursive M,
Unbroken, in graceful collapse, and acceptance
That not all risks reap desired rewards.

Through spring and summer, it remained
Meadow grass enrobing it — green, gold, white

Until it became ragged feathers and shaggy bones
And no buzzards ever came to eat it or bawl over it,
They looked away, seeking sustenance elsewhere.

Not born with the prettiest of faces, it's clear
Life is harder with a shriveled pink skull,
Wobbly and weak claws instead of talons,
Constantly feigning deference to eagles and hawks
Keeping their poker face, awaiting the last word.

Noiseless as they catch thermals in the afternoon sky,
They are not always about eating dead things.
Sometimes they are about flying high for as long as they can
Without moving their wings, for sheer delight of the sky
And the winds that lift them invisibly, alone.

There are screeching times, sure, ground fights, and
Even the dark fate of becoming roadkill themselves.
But all is suspended at dusk when, one by one, they
Drop into layered spirals and land in the redwood tree
Folding their black umbrella wings to end another day.

# Unwept

*Corinne Asturias*

A stanza of confusion bends and twists
Across his forehead — freezing, releasing, freezing
In a futile battle with control
Playing out in slow motion, again
And again, like an alien crash scene
Between a previous version of reality
And a new landscape of unrelenting pain;
His heart a hemorrhage of loss
Of a child, a wife, a life, true love.

Not made for it, perhaps; not taught it, for sure
He stands stranded in the crosshairs of
Certainty and confusion, tall and still,
As his bones threaten to dissolve.
No words can emerge to explain —
No tears can fall to extrude the toxins —
Emotional droplets that might sink
Like fishing weights from heart to earth
But instead embed themselves, throbbing
Swelling, like terrible sores on the soul
While scar tissue builds its unbending sinew, anew.

His eyes move only down, behind, or aside
Straight ahead risks opening the gate:
Rusting the locks, drowning the village.
Like spotlights, his eyes tilt away in furtive arcs

Hooded by the furrow of weighted brows
And lashes that once framed dreams and desires,
Gone for now, maybe for good, blind to any light
Cast from above, invisible to the naked heart.

# Marlene Augustine-Gardini

Marlene retired from the music industry as Senior Director/West Coast Promotion for MCA, a division of Universal Music Group. In her youth she was a member of the award-winning MAGIC CARPET PLAY COMPANY based in San Francisco.

In Sonoma County, she has performed with various readers theatre groups.

Marlene is a writer, and her pieces have appeared in the *California Literary Review* and *Flash Fiction Magazine*.

Marlene's passion is animal rescue especially "TNR", the trapping/neuter/ release of feral cats. After residing for decades in San Francisco Marlene, her husband and their fur of rescues live in Northern California.

# Blueberries

*Marlene Augustine-Gardini*

The diner isn't open yet. Andy fires up the grill and layers slabs of bacon on the back burner. I brew fresh coffee and the smell swirls around and begins to wake up the place.

I put the paper placemats and plastic bottles of maple syrup on the tables and flip the "CLOSED" sign over to welcome breakfast in. Like a clock the old couple comes in. Joined in the middle, arms around each other's waist. I bring them coffee and know their order. I slide the ticket onto the spinner by the pick-up window for Andy.

I turn on the fan. It's August and hot and the fan picks up speed like a kid's pinwheel, forcing the air and the bacon smells down on us.

A couple with a little boy stops inside the doorway, looking for a table. The boy is about five or six.

I'm not good at guessing kids' ages. Or really anything about kids. I mean, I like kids. Andy and I talked about having some once but then we got caught up in wanting the diner and the money we saved went to that and not a wedding. And well... I'd want to be married and stuff... with a kid and all. But we got the diner. Andy calls it "our baby." It's like he said, "we are doing really well with things the way they are." I guess we just got so busy we didn't talk about a family anymore.

The couple with the kid seat themselves by the window. The boy scoots over and puts his hands on the glass. I know I'm gonna have to clean that window when he is gone. Especially if he has pancakes. That's ok. Like I said, I like kids.

I bring two menus for the adults and a plastic cup of crayons and a placemat of Super Heroes and put it in front of the boy.

"You can color this," I say.

And he turns and looks up at me. He has the strangest eyes I have ever seen.

Blue/black, like the berries in the muffins on the counter under the glass dome. Startling color. A bruised, shiny blue outline deepening into the center like liquid coal.

He just stares up at me. Doesn't blink.

"I'm sorry" she says. "Sometimes he doesn't respond."

"That's OK," I say. "That's OK."

The man orders two eggs, over easy, bacon, and toast. The woman orders oatmeal.

"Oh, and a child's pancake with syrup."

I take the order and clip the ticket to the spinner. I look back at the kid.

I think he is looking out the window but he is looking back at me reflected in the glass. Just staring at me. Not blinking. Those eyes, they are like hooks and I'm the fish.

I jerk away and pour more coffee for the old couple, see their order is ready and bring them their poached eggs and buttered toast. I walk past the boy.

He moves his head slightly; his eyes watch me like one of those paintings of Jesus where just his eyes follow you right and left.

Andy taps the bell for pick up. I stack the plates up my arm. Andy leans into the window. "You got all that, kid?" he asks.

"Of course, boss," I say and smile back at him. I bring everything to the booth and put their breakfast down.

I ask if there is anything else.

"No" the man says. "We're good. Thank you."

The boy is looking up at me. The woman cuts up the pancake, pours syrup on it and turns to her oatmeal. The boy picks up a piece of pancake with his fingers and without looking away puts it in his mouth and chews. No one talks. They just eat.

I back away. Lean on the counter by the pick-up window. Andy is looking at me from the kitchen. I wink at him, nod towards the old couple and go give them their bill. They take their time leaving.

I clear their table, drop dirty dishes and silver in the bus tray near the kitchen and turn to check on the family.

The woman is finished eating so I go over and ask if they want anything else.

"No," the man says. "It was fine. Thank you."

I hand him the bill and he gives me a twenty.

"Keep it," he says.

They slide out of the booth. They walk to the door. I look down at the table and the boy has drawn something on the back of the white placemat. Just a dark spot in the center. I pick it up and it looks like a small, dark tear drop. I look closer. It's half of a heart. A blue-black heart with ragged edges torn through the middle.

The boy turns and looks back at me. Andy taps the bell. "No reason," he says when I come to the counter. He smiles, his eyes like the number nine in a paint-by-number kit — oily brown.

"Hey, kid, 'ya doing okay?" he says. I look back at the door. It's still early in the morning. The diner is empty except for us.

I look back at Andy. He is framed in the pick-up window, relaxed and leaning with his arms crossed.

"I guess," I answer. "Yeah, I — I suppose I am."

I fold the paper placemat in half, then in half again. I place it my apron pocket and move to clean the syrup fingerprints off the glass.

# Old Dog Thing

*Marlene Augustine-Gardini.*

"It's an old dog thing," he said.

We were standing in the field behind his house on Christmas Eve, frosted ground crunching like cereal under our feet. Thistle was about ten feet in front of us, staring into the star speckled sky. She was not moving. Just staring.

"I've had her, oh, about 14 years now, ya know," he said. "Some fucker tied her into a plastic bag and tossed her on the side of the road."

"I know, Dad," I said. "She's been a good dog."

He nodded.

"I don't know what made me stop that day, Becks. I'm not like you and your mom always cleaning up the world."

"I know, Dad." I wrapped my arms tighter around my body to throw off the biting air; the L.A. cold didn't run through you like the icy steel blades of Iowa, and no matter how many layers of clothing I wore, I never seemed to get warm here. Dad stood there in just his jeans, with his flannel shirt straining over his girth.

"I hope the mouth of hell opens up and swallows that cocksucker who did that. Burn in hell, the bastard. But, the truth is his evil brought me one damn fine pup. Little thing. She musta been only 10 or 12 weeks old that day. When I undid it, she was just sittin' in the bottom of that bag, looking up at me. Like saying, 'Where you been, Frank? I've been waiting here for ya.' You remember,

13

Becks? I told ya that day 'cause you called. That day I found Thistle? You called that day."

"I remember, Dad. You were so happy. I was happy, too. Someone to be with you."

"Yeah," he said. "I figure your mom sent me to find that bag. Otherwise, I'd just have driven by, ya know?"

I nodded. "Yep, I think she did, Dad. Good thing for both you and Thistle, huh?"

Thistle sat between us, like a small ice sculpture stuck to the ground. The only movement was her breath coming out in tiny puffs of white in the frosty night air.

"Is she okay Dad? Dad? Is Thistle alright? She hasn't moved."

He looked over at me.

"It's an old dog thing, Becks. They do that, they say. Just stare into the sky. She's looking for that tiny crack in the sky where the light comes through. Not the star-light. This…this is different. She knows it's there. When she finds it, well. She'll be gone. It's ok. It's the way it is. She's deaf now, ya know. I remember when she'd be way down the field there and I could just say her name and she'd hightail it back to me. Now, she hears what's inside her I guess."

He walked over to the dog and gently placed his hand on her back. She turned to look up at him, her eyes a cloudy gray. She slowly stood up, leaned into him, and together they walked past me and into the house.

I called each week see how he was. I asked him several times if he had thought of getting another dog. Maybe another old dog just so he wouldn't be alone.

"Don't need another dog, Becks. Not one I'd go looking for. Anyways, if I was supposed to have one it'd find me. Just like she did. I'm fine, hon. Just fine. Don't you worry. Everything is as it's supposed to be. You just take care of you, ok? Your old dad is just fine."

After a while I stopped asking about getting a dog, and we'd talk about the weather and the news, and then it was spring, and we talked about my trip home for Easter.

"Ya really wanna make that trip?" he asked. "Don't need to if ya don't want to. I'm good here. All good. Nights are getting warmer. Pleasant out each night, to say the truth."

"Of course, I'm coming," I said. "I'll be home Friday."

The lights were on in the house when I arrived. I called his name, looking in the living and dining rooms, but he wasn't there. I made my way through the kitchen, and from the doorway I saw him standing in the field. His back was to me, and he was looking up into the sky. It was one of those clean spring nights, and the sky was lit up with white lights, looking like a Christmas tree.

"Dad?" I called. He didn't turn around. I walked closer, calling until finally I was right next to him.

"Dad?"

"Hey, Becks. Look at that, would ya? All of them stars. Could be lightning bugs up there, they go on and off so much. They leave just enough room for a crack in the dark. Just damn beautiful, I'd say. Damn beautiful."

We stood like that for what seemed a few lifetimes, neither of us saying a thing.

I placed my hand on his back and felt the bones under the thin skin. I saw how the shoulder seams on his flannel shirt fell closer to his elbows instead of resting where they should be and how his belt was drawn tightly around his hips. He looked over at me, his eyes soft and smiling.

"It's okay, Becks. It's the way it's supposed to be," he said. "It really is. It's just an old dog thing."

He turned, leaning into me, and together we walked slowly back to the house.

# Stones

*Marlene Augustine-Gardini*

The cemetery gate hung like a hangnail on the rusted post. It had not been closed in a long time. Archangel monuments, once strong and solid, had been set to guard over the graves. But weather and time and drunken party goers had left some of them armless, their raised swords crumbled on the ground like thrown dice. Others stared out over the plots, noseless and with lips worn away like lipstick at the end of a passionate night. Tiny stone angels, hands folded, knelt over postage-size plots, praying eternally for sinless, small souls.

They all stand on ground unkept and forgotten. Those who had wept and erected these memorials were themselves now long gone.

She hurries along the uneven cobble stone path, dirt and rocks ebbing and flowing like a tide. The path abruptly gives way to a gravel path and the dirt becomes golf course green. This is the new section. Ironic for those buried there, she thinks. Some of those who had spent hours in life striving for a manicured lawn now lay underneath that perfection. Green grass; uniform stones like perfect dentures stand row upon row.

She knows she should have come earlier. In the day. In the year. But even on the brightest of bright days, at the best of times this place is not her favorite. Today with clouds the color of worn concrete and cold air wrapping itself around her like the scarf she wishes she'd worn she knows it will be dark soon and she will want to be gone.

For now, it is just her and the stones. Long ago large slabs had been placed on the dirt pile which covered the wooden box that held the body. People had believed placing the stones there would keep the dead from rising. Years later came the pillars of Saints and angels and Christ Himself to stand guard. Finally, someone decided that stones could be set upright, like the headboard on the bed.

She looks around. The grounds look undisturbed. No new occupants.

The earth is damp and she is glad she remembered to bring something this time. She unfolds the towel, places it on the ground and kneels. She brushes the leaves from the base of the stone. The leaves are both dry and wet as if two seasons had joined together, spring and winter, birth and death, green and brown like overlaying mulch.

The lettering is stamped into the stone. Three lines. Filled with dirt. She tries to pry the lines clean with her finger nails but after one chip and one break she decides she knows what it says. No one else who passes by will care.

She looks at the unadorned altar. She bears no gift of flowers, no plants to plant, no mylar balloon that will eventually rip itself free and hurry away, no stuffed animal clutching torn paper hearts with sayings like, "miss you," or "love always." She has seen these things at other cemetery sites and finds it comical to think people believe that the dead take joy in these offerings. She brought no gift to a stone idol.

She misses him. Oh, she does. But not to the extent that she wants to throw herself on the earth that blankets him and sink into the hole that holds him. He is gone. Yet, every so often she comes. Just to see the stone. To read his name. To read the date he came into the world. And the day he left.

The sky has turned more granite than concrete. She brushes a few more leaves away. Places her fingers on the stone after she has raised them to her lips.

She will come again, maybe earlier next time.

She stands up and shakes out the towel. She walks back over the smooth ground, past the identical stones lined up like church pews, back through the jigsaw puzzle of old tombstones. She tugs at the gate but then clasps her hands over her coat to close it instead.

And the night wind kicks up rushing through the tall trees with the sound of running water.

Acorns spill across the graves like broken rosary beads and feral cats slink out of the shadowed mausoleums to dig in the dirt, nature's perfect litter boxes.

Owls swoop silently like souls of the damned to talon the mice that feel brave enough to dance in the fading light.

Rabbits watch the carnage and hug close along the stones.

Gophers tunnel up to eat the stems of the expensive florist's bouquets, the earth spilling around the edges of the inside out graves they make.

In her car she turns up the heater and glances in her rearview mirror at the ghostly stone silhouettes darkening the sky. Her headlights cut into the night.

She hits the gas, racing forward leaving the dead behind, unaware that the place, as it does each night, has come alive.

# Margaret Cullison

A proud Iowan, Margaret has been learning to write ever since her first attempt at fiction as a teenager fell short of perfection. Always an avid reader, she earned a BA in English from Northwestern University.

She writes poetry, fiction and award-winning personal essays. Published nonfiction includes articles about small mammals, birds and backyard water gardens for trade publications.

Margaret's personal essays have been posted on the Senior Women website, and she has also written numerous book reviews for Foreward Magazine.

Margaret is currently writing a fictionalized account of her grandfather's boyhood experiences in the border state of Missouri during the Civil War.

Other creative interests include watercolor painting, playing piano, cooking and genealogy.

cullico82@gmail.com

# First Flight

*Margaret Cullison*

My first memory of my father's interest in flying was when he took me to watch small planes taking off and landing at a grass field somewhere "down the line," as he used to say, from our small town. World War II still raged across the seas, but we Iowans were safe from airplanes that spit bullets and dropped bombs. I remember only a few air raid blackouts, while people who lived on both coasts accepted them as routine. My dad was too old to go to war and thus free to indulge his fascination with flight by watching single engine planes fly, an interest that reflected the growing popularity of general aviation.

I must have been about six years old, standing beside him at the edge of the airstrip. Other plane-watching people stood around us or inspected the airplanes that were tied down in the grass along the side of the runway. We stayed there for a long time, Dad looking skyward without saying much, studying how the flying was done.

The skies over Iowa were clear of both pollution and air traffic. In the clear skies of summer, no radar or navigational instruments were needed. Towards the end of the war, a rudimentary airstrip was built near our town, the rich soil of a cornfield sacrificed for the purpose. One airplane enthusiast was a road engineer who helped lay out the runway. Other men cultivated the remaining corn plants, using the profits from corn sales for airport maintenance.

Dad and I made frequent trips to this airfield closer to home. As before, we stood at the edge of the runway, squinting into the hot sun while a plane glided in for landing. The wings tilted side to side as the pilot adjusted to the changing air currents closer to the ground, a vulnerable package of engine, metal, and human that aimed to land safely on the corn stubble field.

We spent hours watching the pilots doing their "touch and goes." Fierce wind from the propellers blew dust in my eyes and whipped my summer dress against my legs as the planes taxied out. Once, sleepy from standing in the hot sun for so long, I leaned against the man standing next to me, thinking he was my dad. When I looked up, I was shocked to discover that I'd attached myself to an airport regular I didn't know.

Later, a hangar of corrugated metal was built on the field, a long and silvery shed to house the planes. Sun-drenched and hot after our time by the runway, we'd go into the office to get a cold drink. The pop machine opened from the top and the rows of bottles were held in place by their necks on metal tracks. I'd put a nickel in the coin slot and guide my selection along until the cold glass bottle was released into my eager hands. Dad and his friends usually chose the light-colored soda, walked outside to pour some out, the dust fizzing with carbonated liquid, and then added a dash of bourbon. I could never understand why they'd want to waste good pop.

The spring day the war in Europe ended, we drove out to the airport to see what was going on. "Peace. Peace at last," the men all said, as if it were a new word they'd just learned. I guess a lot of soda pop got wasted that day.

A local boy who'd been in the Air Force came home to run the airport and teach flying. He still wore his leather flight jacket with a faded picture of a tiger painted on the back. I called him "funny face," my childish attempt to show my admiration. That municipal airport still operates today with a dozen hangars and two runways, one paved and with lights.

Flush from the post-war economic boom, Dad bought his first airplane, a 1946 cream and red Taylorcraft BC-12D. The interior of the plane smelled of leather. I recall the anticipation stirring in the pit of my stomach as we waited for someone to prime the propeller for us. Then, as the engine roared to life, he'd yell "all clear," waving us on to the airport's runway. We taxied to its end, where Dad went over the safety checklist before taking off. When the wheels left the ground, that first lift into the air felt like magic.

The earth retreated below us. Now surrounded by blue sky, the sun shone blindingly off the nose of the plane. Gradually my ears adjusted to the altitude, the roar of the engine and air rushing over the wings and the fuselage. I looked down at the farms below us, my eyes tracking the highway that led into town. I saw the swimming pool, my school, the downtown square, and finally our house. Dad banked the plane lower as we circled round it. I held tightly to the edge of my seat, looking out the window now almost parallel to the ground. The house looked larger below us. Then he pulled the plane up and out of its turn, dipping the wings. The gold rim of his glasses glinted in the sunlight as he looked towards me, grinning at the fine show we'd put on for the groundlings.

Fifty years later, my oldest brother died. He'd soloed at the age of sixteen and never lost his fascination with flight. In late afternoon, after the memorial service, I saw a plane flying loops and rolls over his house. A long-time friend was in his stunt plane performing aerobatics to honor my brother's memory, with a heartbreakingly stunning show.

Old-time pilots speak reverently of those first post-war private planes like our Taylorcraft, built for the fun and freedom of flying. Dad later bought a single-engine Cessna that he flew frequently on business trips. Sometimes he invited me to join him, choosing me over my two older brothers for this honor. I loved to sit next to him in the cockpit of that remarkable machine as we sped through the air, watching the wispy clouds roll by and gazing down at the lush Iowa farmland. Sometimes the hum of the engine lulled me to sleep, and I woke only when the wheels touched down. Another soft landing that we knew was being critiqued by the plane watchers standing at the edge of the field.

The tradition of airplanes communicating with the earthbound goes on. I still look up and wave when I hear the unmistakable sound of a single-engine plane overhead. It might be too high in the sky for the pilot to notice me, but occasionally I get a jaunty dip of the wings in response.

# The Mud Sculpture — an Iowa Original

*Margaret Cullison*

O n the wall beside my computer hangs a framed photograph of a sculpture that never ceases to inspire me. I first saw it in a tavern in my hometown of Harlan, Iowa. Knowing my fascination with it, my oldest brother had a print made for me.

In the picture, a woman lies with a baby nestled in her left arm, the baby's arm reaching across her breast. Her right arm is outstretched, and the graceful folds of her garment flow over her body in the classical design of a Grecian statue. Mother and child are finely sculpted in every detail.

The full-size figures depict castaways from a shipwreck, and the sculpture is entitled "Cast Up by the Waves." A nineteenth-century novel, of the same name, written by Sir Samuel White Baker inspired the artist's creation. What made this work of art unique is that the woman and baby were sculpted in mud and lie on the earth from which they were created. Within weeks, rain would wash the sculpture entirely away.

The time was April 1929, when the Great Depression had already begun to impact farmers and farm communities in the Midwest. Over-production of crops continued following World War I, even as the need for farm goods dwindled. Crop prices fell, but cost of living increased in the prosperous 20s, and farmers found themselves financially bankrupt.

News about an eccentric artist's arrival in town must have been a welcome diversion from their troubles. The newspaper in Harlan, a rural community of four thousand people in southwestern Iowa, featured two articles about the sculptor.

The first article appeared on the front page and profiled J. B. McCord, who had arrived in town by train and pitched his tent by the railroad tracks. He set to work on his sculpture, ignoring curious onlookers and explaining that he wanted to work alone and free of questions. He kept to himself until the sculpture was finished and then he was willing to talk. McCord said he'd been educated at the Philadelphia School of Fine Arts, but the pressure of working in the critical art world had enervated him and caused health problems. He gave up that stressful life to become an itinerant creator of sculptures in mud.

In other news on the day, a farmer reported finding a wolf's lair while plowing his field and saw two wild eyes peering out at him. A local doctor made a house call to care for a worried couple's infant son. An advertisement pictured men's spring and summer underwear selling from $1.00 to $2.50. Another ad offered a used 1928 Chevrolet Cabriolet, "just as clean as a pin inside and out."

Mr. McCord worked near the water tower that supplied trains passing through town. He used the excess water dripping from the tower to make the mud for his sculptures. A butcher knife was his only tool. Prairie grasses and scrub brush provided a backdrop for his art, and cattails grew in the swampy area below the tracks, closer to the Nishnabotna River. He made two sculptures, one of the woman and child and another of a soldier. Two photographs of the woman and child have been preserved.

The owner of the property where the sculptures lay had tried to persuade McCord to work on his creations in one of the display windows of his store, thereby protecting them from the elements. The artist declined, explaining that he would be too much in the public eye, and the distractions would keep him from doing his best work.

McCord made one ineffective effort to preserve his sculptures by pouring oil over them. A few curious townspeople came to see his work. I wish I knew if my parents, recently married at the time, were among them.

Within a week, spring rain began to wash away the figures, dissolving them back into the earth from whence they came. No one could understand why this talented man didn't care about preserving his work, why he rejected public acclaim, the illusive fame and fortune that often drives creative people. The fact that he completed the work to his own satisfaction must have been enough, art's true worth to him.

He left Harlan as quietly as he had arrived, hopping a train to another town, perhaps with a new subject for his ephemeral art already taking shape in his mind. Other small-town newspapers in the Midwest published stories about his brief visits. His feelings and motivations, the details of his life cannot be known. Despite his desire for anonymity, J. B. McCord's artistic talent has been preserved in those few stories and photographs. But his will to create art for its own sake remains in the photograph on my wall, giving his work a thin thread of immortality.

∽

Grateful thanks to:

The late Gary H. Christiansen, friend and former Mayor of Harlan

*The Harlan Tribune*

The Harlan Community Library

# Return to Aurora

*Margaret Cullison*

My two sons and I chose the weekend of the summer solstice for our trip to the ghost town of Aurora, Nevada, in the high desert east of the Sierra Mountains. Late June in California offered an ideal mix of long days, mild temperatures and vegetation still tinged with the green of winter rain. The foothills stretching ahead of us seemed to glow with the promise of a past we hoped to discover.

Throughout my childhood I heard stories about my mother's great-great grandfather who came to California for the Gold Rush, leaving his wife and five children behind in Ottumwa, Iowa. All that remained of his endeavor were three gold spoons and the enmity of four generations of women who didn't approve of a man who had put his search for adventure and fortune above duty to his family.

Nathaniel Gebhart left Iowa by wagon train in May of 1852. A respected member of his community, he was elected wagon master and steered the group safely to Sutter's Fort by September. He had early success prospecting for gold around Sutter's Fort and the American River, regularly sending money to his wife to sustain their household in Iowa. He came home in 1854, travelling from San Francisco to Panama by steamship, walking across the Isthmus of Panama, where he was robbed of the gold he carried, and then on another ship to New York City and train to Iowa.

This was meant to be the end of his California sojourn. But he had fixed his mind on returning and did in 1855, leaving his wife pregnant with their last child. Nathaniel resumed prospecting along the Yuba River and then around Placerville. Each time he explored a new location, he found only enough gold to keep trying. The great California Mother Lode was by then crowded with prospectors and possibly depleted. Rumors of untapped silver treasures to the east enticed him to consider Bodie and Aurora, nascent boomtowns on the eastern side of the Sierras. With only a pack mule, he walked over the mountains.

Our trip over those mountains took only a few hours in a four-wheel drive. Bodie lies three miles from the Nevada border, a ghost town preserved in an arrested but fragile state of decay by the State of California. Nothing has been done to restore the town, but the walls of the extant buildings have been discreetly shored up, and their windows and roofs reinforced against the severe high desert weather. When we asked park rangers for directions to Aurora, one said the road was nearly impassable and another had never been able to find it.

Stories of the hardy but vulnerable settlers were heartbreakingly evident in the pictures, letters, and newspaper articles we saw on our tour of the museum, which was housed in the old miners' union hall. Some brought their families, and they all endured huge challenges. Temperatures sank below zero in winter and soared to blistering hot in summer. Those few who enjoyed newfound wealth still faced the ever-present danger of sickness, injury, or death.

In one corner of the museum was a small bookstore that featured books about mining life. One that featured Mark Twain's brief time as a prospector caught my eye. When we were about to leave, I went back for a closer look at "Mark Twain, His Adventures at Aurora and Mono Lake" by George Williams III.

Quickly scanning the pages, I stopped short at the sentence, "Man named Gebhart was shot here yesterday trying to defend a claim on Last Chance Hill. Expect he will die." Twain had dreams of striking it rich too and had come to Aurora in early 1862. He wrote frequent letters to his brother, Orion, who financed the venture. Within the next month, Twain had to fight claim jumpers trying to take his own mine. "Now you understand the shooting scrape in which Gebhart was killed the other day," he wrote Orion in one of the letters.

The coincidence of Mark Twain being in Aurora to write about Nathanial's murder and my chance discovery of it over a century later was exciting and fortuitous. The book described precisely how to drive from Bodie to Aurora, crucial information we needed to get there ourselves.

Bodie Canyon Road resembles a dried-up creek bed strewn with boulders and deep mud ruts. We passed a crumbling brick structure that the book identified as the old toll station marking the border between California and Nevada. Making slow, bumpy progress, we stopped near a grove of quaking aspens for lunch from provisions in our cooler. A gentle breeze stirred the aspen leaves, the only sound except for the tapping of an acorn woodpecker further up the canyon slope.

Finally reaching the canyon's end, we turned onto a graded dirt road looking out onto a wide plain scarred by present-day strip mining. Farther east in the hills, we passed the remains of a mill pictured in the book. Nathaniel had been among the first twenty men to arrive in Aurora, and bricks were needed for building the new mining town. He started a kiln that provided income to live on and to finance his mining in hard rock quartz, a process more costly than washing gold out of the placer mines of California.

We passed a sign for the Aurora cemetery, and just beyond that the road opened onto a valley surrounded by rolling hills. The remains of Aurora lay before us. Named "City of the Dawn," by the first settlers, Aurora is a true ghost town. Piles of scattered wooden planks define where buildings once stood, and a single standing concrete wall is the last remnant of the Esmeralda Hotel. Nearly 10,000 people once lived in Aurora, and now only crumbling concrete and rotting wood mark their presence.

Two women, amateur explorers of ghost towns, wrote a book about seeing Aurora in 1935 when over 100 buildings, some made of brick, still stood. The buildings were open to the weather, and they saw walnut and oak furniture and trunks containing old-fashioned clothes and shoes. The walls were still hung with Civil War era calendars. By the late 1940s, scavengers had stolen most of the bricks from those long-deserted buildings and sold them, profiting from postwar construction and the public's passion for old brick.

Nathaniel staked a claim on a silver vein said to be fabulously rich. But fortune still eluded him, and by 1862 he was living in a dugout shack built into the hillside at his mine. The letters he wrote to his wife describe the cold winter he endured in that flimsy dwelling, but he persisted in hoping for success.

In April, claim jumpers attacked, and he attempted to fight them off by brandishing a quartz rock. The principal attacker, a Confederate sympathizer, sought revenge for a heated argument he'd had with Nathaniel about General Grant's recent victory at the Battle of Shiloh. The men carried rifles and shot him in the stomach. He lingered for a few days but died of his wounds at age fifty-two.

A Masonic brother wrote the last letter home, as dictated by Nathaniel as he lay dying. His scrawled signature verifies the content. He asked his wife to forgive him for his selfish obsession with finding gold and declared his love for her.

We decided to leave the town site free of our footsteps and headed up the hill to the cemetery. Situated among pine trees, we walked among the headstones until we found the Masonic section, where our ancestor was buried. We didn't expect to find his grave, knowing it had only been marked by a wooden cross, long since gone.

We sat for a while on the tailgate of the car as the afternoon sun played against the pinyon branches. My great-great-great-grandfather's life ended with sadness and remorse, but we felt content to have returned to Aurora to honor him.

# Amanda Niamh Dawson

Amanda Dawson lives with her husband and children in rural Sonoma County, California. They live on a property of redwoods and oaks, overlooking vineyards and hills towards the Pacific Ocean. Amanda was born in London to Irish and South African parents and then raised in the Boston area. She attended Buckingham, Browne & Nichols School and then went to study Art History and French at Tufts University, the Ecole du Louvre, and Sorbonne University. She worked at Sothebys before joining the editorial team at *House Beautiful Magazine*/Hearst Publishing in New York.

At the same time, her husband pursued his law degree and continued as an MCA recording artist in a jazz/hip-hop band. Years later, relocation to the West Coast to raise their children afforded new opportunities in the antiques trade and styling. Amanda draws inspiration from her parents' stories and recollections of Ireland and from the magnificent California landscape.

# California

*Amanda Niamh Dawson*

Golden light of summer
Fading from our sky
Autumn's softer colors
Come when others die

Birds
They still go swooping
Crying
In the wind

The land has lost its luster
Diggers of gold gave in
Dust has nearly settled
Grass
Smoky and grim

Vines on distant hills
Citrine and garnet strands
Hopeful new arrivals
Transplants by human hand

Blissful wasteland
Left to be

Only place
You feel free

# Sonoma Morning

*Amanda Niamh Dawson*

The thin air of summer
Drifts softly into view
The pine cones
Hang in clusters
Laced with warming dew
Brooms of hay lay nestled
Lining the dusty road
Hillsides burst into blueness
Swept in amber gold
Silence comes in easy
Houses sag their sides
Sunshine filters clouds
Hawks swim on wind tides
Notes of smoke
Stray from fallen leaves in piles
Trees shushing gently
Their branches swish their sleeves
Parted lips
So tender
Wet
With laden breeze

# Wild Nights

*Amanda Niamh Dawson*

On warm nights
My dog has taken to lying by the screen door in the
    bedroom
He listens and watches the darkness

He rises when the cat calls and hoopla of wild coyotes
    stab the stillness
Out into the night, we step together
The cackles haunt a deeper part of us — where we are
    not safe
Where we would be hunted

This dog knows I need him
His purpose, self-prescribed
Some evolution — away from the wildness

The retreating night returns to humming and leaf talk
He resumes his perch
Hearing the silent coyotes
Burrowing in their underground bunker a vineyard away
Wondering
Why they sound like him
And why he's here with me

# Susan E. Gunter

Susan is a Professor of English Emerita. Her poems are published in journals in America, Bulgaria, England, Montenegro, and Sweden. Her poetry reviews have appeared in many journals. Her biography of William James's wife Alice, *Alice in Jamesland,* received an eight-page glowing review in *The New York Review of Books.*

Susan did three Fulbrights in the Balkans, teaching poetry and creative writing.

In 2004-2005, she was a fellow in American literature at Harvard College's Houghton Library. Susan is also an artist. www.susanegunter.com

# Sestina for Esther

*Susan E. Gunter*

The first thing that I remember is a house.
Curved sunbursts circled the long porch
and lilacs shaded the sweet gnarled garden.
At night the house set free its ghosts,
so I hid beneath the covers, keeping still.
They breathed so hard I thought they were in pain.

The old ones in the rooms knew about pain.
They said, in the end, it came to every house.
They said I'd learn someday, but still
I wouldn't believe them. I read on the porch,
fairy stories whose endings were free of ghosts
and whose journeys took me to a far enchanted
   garden.

At twilight, catching fireflies in the garden,
I'd put them in a jar. Was there pain
for them, or were they invincible as ghosts?
After the stars came out I went into the house,
leaving the mayonnaise jar on the porch.
In the morning all the fireflies were still.

Mason jars lined the cellar shelves, distilled
brandy, cherries, spiced peaches from the garden.
Against the stone wall the striped canvas porch
swing rested from summer storms. Discarded pain

remedies were thrown beneath the stairs. The house
swayed above those restless moaning ghosts.

I wish I'd stop dreaming about those ghosts.
I wish that my mother were still
in the kitchen, baking bread in the house
and canning the wealth of her late summer's garden.
I wish she had withstood the pain
that made her jump from a beam on the porch.

All their warnings came true on the porch.
Then I knew what the old ones meant. The ghosts
had condemned her to a twilight world of pain.
After she jumped, all their voices were still.
Weeds choked her yellow roses in the garden
and the white paint peeled from the house.

# Riding the Amtrak, Cary N.C. to Alexandria VA

*Susan E. Gunter*

It's all one long crime scene out my window    a country
   made of cold crimes

my eyes scan the wayside like vultures waiting to pick the
   bones of the dead
seeing the cruelty of trees leaning into one another because
            some of us bear weight and some of us are
            the weight
other trees standing upright muzzle-loading rifles
        or sentinels keeping the watch over
        ruined dreams

that color should make such a difference when it's poured
   over pigment

passing TW's Antique Mall one erect black man standing
   at an angle to an old white
        man leaning on a cane
no eye contact   we're in Selma but it's not Alabama
   and the church always the church

or it's the Wilson railway station where a pack of six
   young men idles at its side
        one in an orange hoodie all in ear buds

no full employment here in Wilson     while at Warren
   Wilson other unemployeds write
      poems about them they'll never read     because they
      can't    can't read that is
        and oh my god this country's rotten to the core

we're sharecropping the world bingo you lose it's the
   lottery of life
      this is no utopia buddy just the Great Dismal
      Swamp where watersnakes
spawn and no birds sing    and oh gentle jesus that
   junkyard of cars stretches out to the
                    crack of doom

Mary mother of god be with us now and at the hour of
   our death

# At the Harding Glacier

*Susan E. Gunter*

*One must have a mind of winter.* — Wallace Stevens

We steam in
on diesel power, into
the very heart of light,
like Poe's Pym.

When the engines stop
We walk on deck to watch
the glacier calve into
the blue hard sea.

We burn in this cold air,
listening to the seracs
beat the water into sprays
of odorless ice flowers.

This tune of hollow misery
sounds like nothing
we can name, contrabassoons
playing in a key of doom.

Click. Click. Click.
Glacial ice spikes
our drinks, turning us
into snowmen.

When eggshell shadows
climb the crevasses,
the sun slips and
the air drops to zero.

We steam away,
the glacier stalking us,
reminding us that
all our narratives
have the same ending.

# Judith Hardenbrook

Now in her 70s, Judith was raised on the east coast in an artistic family.

She is a self-taught fine artist, gardener and traveler. She lived in Maine and now California wine country is home.

This year she was inspired to write poems, generally on the light side.

Judith says, "I smile as I write them."

# The baboon, an aspiring musician

*Judith Hardenbrook*

*lived in New York's Central Park Zoo*

In the evenings,
He saw the women
In fancy dresses,
And men in tuxedos
Walking by,
Chattering,
Humming,
Or calling a cab.
Saying
"Take me please
to Carnegie Hall,"
For a concert.
Conducted
Someone famous,
With an un pronounceable name.

The baboon
Dreamed one day
Of singing there.
But he knew
He couldn't
Stand on the stage alone.
He needed
Musical accompaniment.

In the cage next to him,
His friend the penguin
Would conduct.
He had the outfit already,
As though conducting
Was always his destiny.
All he needed was
The conductor's black wand.

The tortoise wanted to harmonize
But wasn't tall enough.
So he asked the tiger
Nearby,
If he could stand on him.
The tiger agreed
But was still not tall enough,
The tiger asked the zebra.
"May I stand on you?"
The zebra replied,
"Too many stripes
And claws much too sharp."
Instead the tortoise
Found a seat
On the hippo's head,
Nice and wide.

The monkey asked if he could come.
The only wild animal
with opposable thumbs,
He chose the drums.

He could hold the sticks.
Rat-a-tat-tat.
His playing was bold.
Rat-a-tat-tat
On the drums.

The squirrel lived at the Zoo, too,
But not in a cage.
One day,
Passing the Zoo's cafe,
She turned
Went in,
Leaving with spoons.
She'll play them soon
On the Carnegie stage.

The little koala standing tall
On the camel's hump
Would play the triangles,
A clear, tinkling, vibrating sound.
The graceful gazelle
Chose the bells.
The rhino wanted to play the violin
But that instrument was too small.
So he choose the bass
And held it under his chin,
The toucan flew the bow back and forth.
The sound mimicking
The low rumble

Of the jungle
At night.

The bear, the goat, and the hippo,
Of the Delacorte clock
At the edge of the zoo
Loaned the new musicians
Their instruments
Instructing them,
Tapping out the melody.
Louder, now softer,
Wrong note
Oh! The goat
Ate the pages of music again,
Oh my!
Play anyway.
The Delacorte musicians said.
You know the notes,
Simply play!

Friday night,
The concert was scheduled,
The grizzly bear led the way,
Clearing the path
For the Zoo musicians,
Marching,
Passing the Plaza Hotel,
Down Fifth Avenue,
Past Tiffany's
On the way to Carnegie Hall

For the debut performance
Of their symphony
"Wild in New York City".

The kangaroo gave out the music
She kept in her pocket.
The parakeets turned the pages,
But couldn't stop twittering.
So flute playing the butterflies
I asked the spiders to turn.
They spun their cobwebs from the ceiling
And with their multiple legs
Could turn six pages at a once.

The peacock came,
But was told not to sing.
His voice was frightful.
"Please stand to the side.
Spread your tail and look beautiful.
Smile, don't sing."

The worrisome python stretching
Across the stage
Kept the beat with his tail.
The baboon stood in front.
The penguin conductor
Took his place on the podium.
Raising his beautiful new wand,
Signaling the baboon to begin,
He sang.

Nervous at first,
But then,
He sang with his heart.
"Start spreading the news,
We're from Central Park Zoo,
Delighted to be here,
To sing and play for you.
Bringing the soul of our jungle homes
To you
"Wild New York."

The audience was quiet,
Hands folded,
Listening,
Then erupted in
Swoons of amazement,
Their own baboon baritone.
Their simian Pavarotti.
They gave
The animals, birds and reptiles
A standing ovation.
They couldn't stop clapping

On the stage the baboon
Bowed and thanked the audience
For giving them a chance to sing for them.
That evening
The flamingo
Was recruited by the Balanchine Ballet
To dance

In the famous ballet,
The Nutcracker.
She'd be the first snow queen
All in pink to solo.

The ostrich was given a job
With the Rockettes
Her legs were so long
And she already had the feathers.

The animals were happy
And left through the back door.
The elephant was there.
He had marched
With them
To Carnegie Hall
But the doors weren't made for elephants
So he waited.

Through the black, starless night
The elephant
Carried them all
Home to the zoo,
All save the birds who flew
Themselves home.
The breeze blew
A cloud over the moon.
The stars flittered.
It was dark
As they slipped

Into their cozy cages,
The musicians softly roared,
Neighed, growled
Or chirped
Saying "Good Night."
Drifting to sleep,
Dreaming the tunes of the night.

It was a wonderful night!

# Sheila Jones

Originally from NYC, Sheila spent her younger years in music, art, and writing.

A member of "The Group Image Ent. Inc.," she was the singer in "The GI Band."

In 1968 she released "A Mouth in the Clouds" on Community Records.

Since 1969, she spent many years in Mexico and California, incorporating music and writing with her life.

Sheila is passionate about archeology, anthropology, history, indigenous cultures, diving, horses and writing.

# China

*Sheila Jones*

I live in China
Working in a factory
Making plastic sheets
For plastic technology
Surgical mask
Protect my ass
I'm so homesick
Hope to pass
My time in a better way
Living in a new way
I live in China
Like a bull in the China shop
I make the plastic
To wrap on the tabletop
Where computers, toys
Weapons or shoes
Bags and chips
No union dues
I live in China
But not like a rock
I work in the factory
Checking the stock
My baby has an iPad
Right on his diaper
That's how we know
If his life will be brighter

I live in China
But my heart's in America
Or maybe it's Mexico
Maybe Mayan
What's yours
What's the same
Is the plastic
The poison burns thick
Can not choose
With the mask I pick
I live in China
But my heart's in the world
My feet in the ground
Time to go round
Please make my plastic
Sheet custom fit
So I'm safe and comfy
In my Pacal ship
Ship me in
Or ship me out
I live in China
And I can't get out

# Yaxunah

*Sheila Jones*

Is time killing me
Or am I killing time
Out to that magic place she goes
Dancing on those ancient stones
Set to the sun
Father sky
Mother Earth
The four directions
The spirit all around us
She sits and closes her eyes
Everything turns bright red
Ringing sounds of brilliant colors
She raises both hands to the sun
The clouds gather in the sky
Grey blue and white
Running and blending into each other
A lightning bolt separates the sky in two
Silently
Baby Raw Thunderbolt
Popol Vuh Hero Twins
Will we save the Earth
Is it too late for the Earth to save us
She goes down that Mayan Road
In the old white pickup
The Earth is steaming
Vapor rising

As dew drops on her arm
Resting on the doorframe
Of the truck
The trees are bowing
Framing the road with its flowers
Blessing begging
Her soul back to that ancient place
In your heart
Oh to be human
To smell the rain and the misty red Mother Earth
Oh the gift of humans
How we can have our senses
How we can create
How we can pray to that spirit
She is humbled
She is dumbfounded
Bow down to the mighty spirit
Foot to stone
Count the time
What are we in this universe
Hold on it's spinning
Speeding up
Dance on the ancient temple
Round to the East
Round to the West
Round to the North
Round to the South
Watch out
Here it comes
Hammering rain

Mother Nature is crying
She is suckling the Milpas of corn
Reaching to the sun
Over and over and over again we go
Spit us out and chew us up again

# Turn Around

*Sheila Jones*

Turn Around
We were shining
Young beautiful and bold
The days of our youth behind us
Left in a blaze of glory

I turned around and looked for you
I looked on the stage
And I looked in the park
I turned around and I looked for you
In the avenue of protest
In the music store of our town

I turned around and I looked for you
In the back door rooms filled with cigarettes
And low filtered music

I turned around when we were there
So young
So strong and fearless
So beautiful and perfect in our madness of song
And revolution

I turned around and I looked for you
In the streets and bars
And the colleges of students of invention

I turned around and looked for you
On the battlefields of ignorance and hate
In the houses of faith and longing

I turned and looked for you
Where the microphones made feedback
And the plastic cup was wet and dripping
Along the electric cords
That wrapped around my feet
And plugged into my brain

I turned
I thought we had changed the world
I turned
I thought we had learned something new
I turned
I thought we had gotten older
I turned
I thought we had a better mind

I turned and I looked for you
In the same battlefield in Kosovo
In the same battlefield as Columbine
In the same battlefield in my heart
That lies broken in despair of disappointment
How could we make such a world

I turned around and looked for you
And only saw myself

# One Day in the Yucatan

*Sheila Jones*

It was another beautiful morning. Sun rising, cool out. She loved to travel on the roads. Today she would make her usual run to Carrillo Puerto with an extra task in mind. There was a small nursery on the way where she just might find a tree called Lluvia de Oro (Rain of Gold) known for its beautiful blooms of hanging golden flowers. Looking like tears of gold. They were hard to find and do not always flower. If you plant one and it flowers, it's a fortunate blessing.

She was driving her brand new white Ford Ranger pickup. It seemed like anything was possible. It was about an hour and a half each way. She stopped at the little nursery and got lucky. She was able to buy a sturdy young tree. She lifted it to the bed of the truck and used the soga (rope) to secure it so it wouldn't fall over during the bouncy ride. She continued to Carrillo, tree in tow. First stop in town was her favorite restaurant. It wasn't fancy but had good clean food. You have to be super careful with water and food. You absolutely cannot drink anything but Agua Purificada (bottled water). All fruits and veggies have to be washed and soaked in water that has microdyne disinfectant drops. This place was safe. Always order the same thing. A liquado (shake) of papaya with two shots of rum, quesadillas, stuffed with pico de gallo. (Salsa with chile), and fried bananas with cream. Yum. Next stop at the market. All the local vendors selling fruit, fresh tortillas, fresh cheese, every kind of chile, and beautiful flowers. White lilies, Gladiolus, and her favorite Sussanas. The small white buds smelled sweeter and stronger than jasmine. She packed up her large sturdy plastic market bag. Placed it in the passenger seat in her new spotless powerful truck. Stopped for gas and on the road for home. The day was rapidly passing by. As she was approaching the ancient city of Tulum, she saw something blocking the road. It looked like a red car, that crashed into the edge of the jungle upside down. A man with a Volkswagen was trying to help. Something was going on for sure. There was no one else on the road. Suddenly the man with the Volkswagen came running towards her helping a woman covered in blood. She understood that she had to help her right away. Putting a jacket around her she helped her into the truck. Carrillo Puerto was the closest hospital. In those days there were no cell phones, no 911. It was the way things were. When someone was hurt, you helped them. So, that's what she did. Turn that brand new sparkling clean Ford Ranger pick up around with her passenger covered in blood, back for the hour and a half drive. The woman was slumped over. She was trying to keep her patient awake. Open her eyes, talk. Where was she from? What was her name? Please stay alive. The woman was asking for her baby over and over and over again. In those fast moments of saving lives the man with the Volkswagen took the baby. He was following right behind them. She was worried. What if the man decides to keep the baby? She had no time for stupid thoughts. Just continue as fast as she could to save this woman. After an hour or so she arrived at the hospital. People came to help the patient out of the truck. She was so glad they made it and she was alive. After the man in the Volkswagen arrived with the baby, it was time to return home Whew. That was intense. Down the road again. After an hour she approached the outside of Tulum. The car that had crashed was more visible. There was a man's body lying in the road. The body was twisted and absurdly deformed in an almost inhuman position. She stopped and talked to the Officer that had finally arrived. The man sadly was the woman's husband and father to the baby. He had died. They were on vacation from Puebla. One of the tires exploded while they were driving. The car crashed and flipped over upside down. She spoke with the Officer and explained that she had brought the woman to the hospital in Carrillo, and the baby was taken there as well. Slowly she got back in her sturdy white Ford Ranger pickup and started driving with her Lluvia de Oro, fruit and veggies, fresh cheese, homemade corn tortillas and a bloody jacket that helped to save a woman's life. She thought back to that crucial moment on the road. Was she really that kind of person that would worry more about getting blood all over her brand new truck? Was she really that kind of person? No absolutely not.

Years later she was resting at home when the phone started ringing. She picked it up as an unknown voice asked for her by name. "This is Sylvia, the woman whose life you saved about five years ago. I have been looking for you for so long. I found out you lived in Puerto and you had that big white Ford Ranger pickup. I've been waiting all this time to thank you. All my family thanks you, my friends and neighbors. I cannot believe I finally found you." I asked how her baby was. He was fine. Unfortunately, her husband passed away that day. She never thought about that incident. Saving this woman's life. It was simple. The law of the road. You just helped people when it was possible. It was special that Sylvia lived. Her baby lived. It made her feel warm inside. This woman made a huge effort to find her and thank her. It surely was a blessing that she had her brand new powerful Ford Ranger white pickup that day. Almost as if its solitary purpose was to be there, that moment, in time, and in their lives.

# *Corrida de Torros* Tacab 1992 Yucatan

*Sheila Jones*

On the 23rd of July she was invited to a Fiesta in a small Mayan village. It's located on the road to Merida from Carrillo Puerto. This Mayan village had been unchanged for hundreds of years. Each road leads to the center of town (the *zocalo)* where the church is. All the walls and fences are made of rock, piled high and thick. The rocks were from dismantled ancient Mayan temples. The church was built with the same rock. She couldn't help immediately notice the gigantic mango trees, flowers and cocos. Every single Mayan *milpa* was in perfect order and harmony with nature.

The festival was the *corrida de toros*, the showing of the bulls, with live music after. It was incredible. First her friend took her to the church to give thanks and blessings. There are many Saints. Probably two for every day of the year. So, there are always fiestas and celebrations. This one was for *Santa Elena,* who is the patron saint of this village. The ritual was the bullfighter had to enter the church and pray to the idols for protection from the bull.

There are actually three villages that make up the Pueblo of 8000 people, that have been here for generations. The homes are modest *palapas*, mostly designed and constructed by the natural resources of the jungle. The foundations are made of carefully hand cut stone called *Vista Maya*, the walls made of *nacaz* wood, the *techo* roofs made from hand woven palm called *quano*, a thicker leaf.

She felt like her heart would explode from the beauty, and the honor of the people. To her there is no great mystery as to where the Maya went. You can see that they are still here living in the same traditional villages. They travel five hours by bus during the week to the tourist area, where they work as laborers sleeping at the site all week. On the weekends they return home and bring their pay. It was quite an experience to be invited to their town period. As she walked down the narrow dirt paths to the *zocalo*, there were different vendors selling everything from clothing to sweets, white corn on the cob, steaming hot, dipped in cream, sprinkled with the grated cheese, topped with red chili double yum. The band was setting up their scaffolding and sound system for the dancing that would go all night.

When she arrived at the rodeo she was amazed. The arena was made of the same local *nacaz* wood with fresh green large palm leaves. Bleachers and seats were all made by the local town people just for the occasion. The horses were from local villages, the absolute best. There were a bunch of riders and horses as we approached. There was one girl among about ten men. Each horse was beautiful and well trained. The bulls were raised to being controlled by the horses. They would back up the truck carrying the bull to the shoot at the entrance to the arena. The cowboys would ride into the center ring with a full gallop, and then the bull is released into the ring. There were five matadors that she could see, but it all happened so fast. You couldn't tell what was going on. The matadors were wearing very plain clothes. Nothing like the fancy outfits from Spain.

They had no protection, no shields, no swords. At each of the corners of the arena there were cubby holes where the matadors could run and hide. They were made of plywood. Not very strong. When the horses left the arena the bull entered. Immediately the matador started shouting trying to get a reaction from the bull. Each one had a red or yellow rag that they moved and taunted the bull with. The bull casually walked by, when one of the matadors right in front of her, started moving towards the protected area. The bull turned around, looked right at this man, or right at her it felt like, and charged a direct line right at the matador. Within seconds the bull had rammed the man against the fence and pierced his stomach through with his horns. He then flipped the man into the air and onto his back. Then he charged again throwing the matadors body around like straw. Hammering the poor man to the ground he thoroughly stomped his body with all his weight and power. At this point everyone was screaming. It happened directly in front of her. After what seemed like forever but was only a matter of seconds, the other matadors came over and distracted the bull, while the wounded man was taken to safety. The cowboys came out again trying to entertain the crowd. There was a beautiful grappled grey horse that loved to dance. A girl on a white smaller horse riding with the tall handsome young man on a larger horse. Two young men came riding in on fast brown horses whose whole job was to try and knock their opponent off his saddle. Another rider just liked to drink his beer and show off his beautiful mount. None of that mattered because the matador was still alive and she wondered what his thoughts would be. Glad that he would die in the arena by the spirit of the beast that he admired? Did he say goodbye to the person he loved? or his children he would never see again? pray to Santa Elena to take his soul to heaven so close by? Her Mayan friend said he lost his faith. Which means when you fight the bull and don't go into the church you lose. Everyone was giving thanks and thinking of Santa Elena, whose day had come into full celebration. The show went on, another bull was released but there was too much fear in the air. Each time the bull would come near, the matadors would drop their rags and retreat behind the security areas. The horses came in and escorted the bulls out of the arena

She heard a Mayan woman say "tell your friends to stop throwing glass beer bottles from the stands, the children can get hurt." A lady in front of her turned and said the matador had died. Her eyes moistened with tears, and she silently prayed for his soul. Everyone was affected. He had been the best. The matador who killed the bulls. By the end of the day, they had already killed ten more. As in Maya style, as soon as a bull was killed, he went straight to the little butcher stand and was cut up for meat to sell. Nothing was wasted. Children are exposed to facts of life. Blood, bullfights, responsibility, and faith in God. All like a guarded secret known only to the Maya for thousands of years. This was not a tourist show. This was her being invited by respect, by fairness and trust. Equality.

About a week later she was invited again. But this time it was utter devastation. It had rained hard in the village, and then the electric cable line had disconnected from the transformer. Her friend's beautiful 15-year-old son ran out barefoot to tell his father he had received a phone call. As he ran, barefoot, wet hair, from bathing, he accidentally stepped on the open cable, immediately killing him.

Yes life is fragile, with no guarantees.

# Chuck Kensler

Chuck Kensler is an award-winning author, storyteller, and infrequent actor. His short stories and essays have appeared in literary journals, newspapers, on stage, and radio. Many of his stories are based on Lakota Sioux oral traditions.

Chuck received the Ellen Meloy Scholarship Award for social change, and his favorite pastime is to watch his pinot noir grapes grow in Sebastopol.

# Whisker Pluckers

*Chuck Kensler*

The Cheyenne River Indian Agency is near Mobridge, South Dakota. Grandfather has lived on this monotonous reservation all his life. He'll be waiting for me. I figure it's easier to visit a caged animal than to be one.

Will I remember any of my forgotten Sioux words? such as *Tunkasila* for Grandfather.

Yes. *Tunkasila*. In Sioux thought, *Tunkasila* means "the oldest creation who is precious to me." I best remember *Tunkasila*.

The rutted road flings gravel at the sky, and dust twists and tumbles behind my bump-along rattletrap. Then I remember those roadside Burma Shave signs. How about: "**If you think / She likes / Your bristles / Walk bare-footed / Through some thistles / Burma Shave.**" What a laugh. Indians don't shave, especially full bloods. We're whisker pluckers.

Tumbleweeds grab the agency sign like wind witches. The direction arrow is tilted down and points at the sticky blue gumbo. Along the jerky reservation road, the first shave sign spells out **If you think**. I drive through creek water. And on the next rise **She likes** waggles in the wind. A sign that should say **Your bristles** seems to be missing like a swiped bike. It should be on that buckle of land but probably was blown into Minnesota. The next sign is a magpie perch, and under the bird's whitewash, the black letters read **Walk bare-footed.** Just beyond a broken buckboard is a **Through some thistles** sign. Then the last sign—**Burma Shave**—is near a clutter of agency buildings, rickety shacks, leaning outhouses, junked cars, and flies circling ratty piles of no-good throw-aways.

The road peters out in a clearing where Grandfather lives in a cobbled-chicken coop. The walls are chinked with years of mud and tatters of stuffed rags and newspapers. The roof is a scramble of willow sticks, sun-warped boards, tar paper, and . . . and—I'll be damned— a black-lettered sign **Your bristles**—held down with bald tires and layers of dust.

A bone-thin dog sleeps in the shade of the squaw cooler made with skinned sticks. Grandfather looks in a cracked mirror hanging from a cottonwood branch. He's a sepia-tinted photograph. His hair is a long drift of snow.

"*Hau kola*, Sonny. Thought you'd be here today. I'm working on my face. Coffee's hot on the fire. Pour me some too." He talks in the Sioux way—a few words are pushed out his nose as the French do it—like a poorly hummed song. Familiar words singsong as he talks—stories he started two years ago. We drink double-boiled coffee from tin cups.

His cloudy eyes search the mirror for bristles here and there on his nearly hairless face. "Thought I'd fancy up," and he feels with his knotted fingers and cuts a whisker from his chin with a double-edge razor blade. Then another and another. "Clean up this whisker-bed before I'm a broom." Then I watch his tweezers pluck short gray stubble from his leather-brown jaw. How does he decide which bristles get cut and which ones get plucked?

His father taught him how to pluck with a splinter of wood. Sometimes he plucked with a clamshell. When I was too-thin-to-throw-a-shadow kid he used copper tweezers to pull out his scraggly whiskers. I learned long ago not to laugh at his stories about how he got dolled up by plucking his eyebrows into thin lines and painting his face before tying on his war bag and riding with Sitting Bull.

I wonder if he would have been as famous as Crazy Horse if his name wasn't Lazy Horse when he says, "Sonny, I patched roof hole that dripped rain and sifted dirt. Fixed with wood sign I found along the road down by the Moreau River. Enough signs there to fix leaks for the rest of my life." He cuts and plucks some more.

"Sonny. Got another roof hole. Needs a patch. Want some more black medicine? Pour me a cup, too." Grandfather plucks whiskers from under his nose.

I sip *pejuta sapa* and answer, "*Lila waste yelo, Tunkasila,*" this tastes real good, Grandfather.

I wonder if we should arrange the Burma Shave roof patches so they can be read in sequence. But it doesn't matter; Grandfather says he can't read black talking marks.

# Final Rejection

*Chuck Kensler*

Virgil White Weasel pulls the envelope from his mailbox, and wonders if it is a letter of acceptance or one filled with the hollow words of rejection. Perhaps his latest submittal, the one concocted with his estranged wife in mind, and titled *The Ragged Edge*, is more wrong-headed than he meant it to be. He thrusts the unopened letter into the top pocket of his bib overalls and speculates, what if it isn't a rejection letter?

Virgil has learned his rejection lessons well. He thinks about Angie as he trudges back home through a straggle of makeshift shacks scattered here and there like lost buttons, marking the time when the town died and his neighbors gave up and left. And Angie left too, shortly after the baby was born—during the messy divorce.

The *Dupree Sentinel* reported, "irreconcilable differences." Angie's mother in her hissy whisper said "miscegenation." Virgil felt strange when he wrote thin-stretched thoughts about "uxoricide," into the last chapter about "Rejection in Three Easy Steps." Then his mind exploded into a pile of loose hay.

At the end of the dusty road, a shiny city Cadillac is parked between Virgil's cobbled house and a patch of thistles. A slick-haired man—one of those gangster-sorts who

75

mumbles 'dees,' 'dems,' and 'does'—waits in the car and smokes a ready-made cigarette while he finger-pinches sharp creases in the legs of his pinstriped suit. Virgil slips into the kitchen's smell of double-boiled coffee mingled with heliotrope perfume. Virgil knows Angie is there.

Her soiled satin high heels make her somewhat wobbly. She brushes aside a wisp of her now-red hair. Virgil eyes her smudged mascara. He remembers her old sweat, and wonders if she's always been shaped like New Hampshire.

Virgil nods at Angie. He hasn't seen her in over two months since she'd run off to the big city to be with her highfalutin cousin, Myrt, who told Angie, "We ain't got no Dust Bowl in Chicago," and Angie left—left the baby, too.

Angie stands like a nervous bird and makes twitching eye blinks. Her lopsided smile reveals red-smeared lipstick on a front tooth. She seems to peek upward to see if the sky is still there, then says, "Lo, Virg. Ain't too gooda day is it? Waddyathink, Virg, waddyathink?"

"You're right, Angie. It's not a good day. C'mon. She's in the other room."

Angie follows Virgil's curled finger.

A narrow stream of sunlight angles through a tear in the window shade and casts a splinter of light on the table where the baby lies. It's the kind of light Jesus always seems to sit under. There isn't money for a coffin so she's in a pasteboard box.

Her best clothes are carefully arranged, as one would dress a doll for a tea party. A thin pink ribbon is tied around her neck as she lies perfectly still. Not a breath. Her quiet sleep. She never had a chance to grow old enough to throw chicken peck-food.

Virgil pulls an eagle-bone whistle from his pocket and places it near the baby's hand. He tucks a twist of sweet-grass under her feet. He touches her hair, then her cheek. He lays the unopened letter in the box, and ties the lid closed with white butcher string.

In a strange, edgy voice Virgil murmurs, "Angie, that's Step 2."

The time for Step 3 has come. No words are spoken as Virgil's liver-colored hand grabs Angie's slender white hand and leads her out the back door.

# Wanaga ta Caku

*Chuck Kensler*

I open my eyes. I've been here before. I won't come back. The morning sky pushes the night stars away. The spirit trail of *Wanagi ta Caku*—the Milky Way—fades into morning light. The heaven of fireflies will hide until another day's end. The owl warns me I will be under the spell of the stars and moon at the time when blueberries are gathered. And my dreams lead me to the edge of my life.

I close my eyes. The Moon When Turnips Bloom is the time Sitting Bull and Crazy Horse prepare our people to defend our sacred land against Long Hair's horse soldiers. We will face this man called Custer and his blue coats during the Moon When the Wild Roses Bloom. My war bag is ready. My paint will protect me: forehead as yellow as squash skin, black covers my eyes from ear to ear. My *sunka wakan* is more powerful with my black handprint on his rump and his tail tied for war.

I open my eyes. My pony lies on top of me—his lather dries under a clay-yellow sun. His rib blood oozes from a shot hole. Heaves of broken wind and small shudders tell me we will no longer ride together. I blink at the sky. I feel sharp pieces of shattered bone. I taste my blood, salty as *wasna*—dried meat for long journeys. I see my blood dark as chokecherries when ocher dust lies on the baked earth.

I close my eyes. Long Hair stands among his dead. I ride toward him to steal his spirit. Our eyes meet and we see brave warriors. His eyes are steady. My eyes show him my *tiospaye*—my family who went before me and those who will follow. I will have honor and wear an eagle feather for counting coup before Long Hair's deathblow.

I open my eyes. The ember-white sun moves across the clear sky. My pony has left me—gone with his brown-spotted back—paw prints of the wild dog. I squeeze my eyes tight against the pain and see sparks of white stars. I send my voice out and know that by enduring pain something else will not have to suffer. I hear the spirit force of my people's words mingle with the soldiers' cries of death.

I close my eyes. The air is dust and smoke filled with gunpowder and battle. I smell sage and a braid of sweet grass. Dried tobacco blossoms. Onion grass and green hazel burs. I smell bloodroot dye my mother uses for quilled pouches. I smell death and my own smell.

I open my eyes. An ant carries a green bead from my broken armband. It moves through brittle, two-day grass to hide my bead in its sandy hill. My family collects my weapons, food, and clothing for my journey. I will walk the spirit trail across the heavens—back to when the mole was sharp-eyed and the crow was white.

I close my eyes. I've been here before. I won't come back.

# George Korolog

George Korolog is a writer/poet who moved to Sebastopol after a forty-year career in the technology business in Silicon Valley. He has twice been nominated for a Pushcart Prize. He has had his work published in the *Los Angeles Review, Naugatuck River Review, Chiron Review, Southern Indiana Review* and *Tar River Review* among many others.

George's work is included in a number of anthologies. His two published books of poetry are: *Raw String* by Finishing Line Press and *Collapsing Outside the Box* by Aldrich Press.

Gkorolog@gmail.com

# A Response to the Woman who Played with Herself (and God)

*George Korolog*

You had me from the moment you dared to enlighten me,
that sweet smile dangling over the edge of your bright
pink Cosmopolitan,
your face teetering at the wrong angle,
but not the words, which were never slanted
nor the slightest bit out of position.
You mentioned it almost as an aside, in the simplest way,
said that you masturbated in the dark,
in the Hindu way,
with one eye on God and the other just below the hairline
where church was held.
Said it in an effortless small sentence, with a straight face,
as if you were announcing publicly
that you were a Lutheran or a Catholic,
then moving on to the feta and pear appetizer.
Your straightforwardness gave the world a legitimacy
that I would normally assign to the certainty
of natural processes such as sunrises and sunsets.
You didn't elaborate any further, so I imagined you
with your hands between your legs, signing with God,
one finger at a time, asking for forgiveness
and demanding satisfaction simultaneously.
I thought it was sweet revenge to think
that you were teasing Him

in the same way that He teased us every day,
not quite getting us there, but promising more to come
if we only kept going. I saw it right away.
Talking with God was a slow and delicate process,
with its own lessons.
One should never trust the outcome of too much,
too fast, even when it feels good
and we think of it as Holy.

# December, California

*George Korolog*

The trees are still thinking
in the unbreakable air,
snapping grey,
leaving strands of intuition
across the line of
the horizon, the bruised sky,
thoughtfulness hanging
gossamer on the rising
tip of the crescent moon.

The leaves are as hesitant
as my heart can make them,
"do not fall," I say, but they
dream of the beautiful
starkness of their forfeit,
forgiving everything,
absolving the world, a
confessional of root and vein.

The winds consider these
things, the relinquishment
of sin and the purpose of
letting go, licking the nearly
barren trees without judgment,
their gusts, tonguing the
peeling bark in a last kiss.

# Believing in Furniture

*George Korolog*

A thing is a thing. What could be more obvious?
It is named and it becomes.
    When it is not named it becomes anyway.
It becomes something
     and nothing,
then everything.
Let's call it a tabletop,
   flat or not so level,
      varnished or unfinished,
a wedding gift,
a project,
   something made in the garage,
three legs,
   four legs,
     legs with gouges
      from dog teeth,
a showcase for books, magazines,
a place to separate stems from seeds.
When it becomes something more,
     I give it a new name.

I name it more and less.

A favorite table top,

a family heirloom,

a support for her back so I can press down.

Hard.

Something becomes more.

The name becomes more.

I become more.

The table top becomes more.

I see it and say, "see, this is a table top.

Watch it become."

I know this in same way that I know that leaves fall in
 Autumn,

that they become piles,

but eventually becoming shade again.

One day,

the table top will be named trash or fire,

but today

it is polished wood with lacquer.

How can something be other than what it is named?

When it becomes,

I confess to what I see.

I tell it what I believe in.

I tell it that it has become my religion.

# Eschatology

*George Korolog*

It is all moving
in the same direction,
and so, it seems
that remembering
yesterday's point,
the argument
or the confession
does nothing to hinder
forward motion.
It's an inexorable slide
into sickness or tragedy
and no thought can hold
permanence
unfolding,
for everything you see
is in the past.

# Southern Exposure

*George Korolog*

The mountain reveled in its explicit smokiness, with a glare that was not nearly as natural as it was exclusionary. Never took to strangers. Coming down the backside, on my way to see Mom's people, I could feel the lazy misgivings of the sun grimacing on the surface of the Ocoee as I wound my way south through sleepy towns with names like Murfreesboro, Tullahoma and Thomson's Station. Going to visit the family. Family with names like Ezra, Flossie Mae, Mildred, Everett, Grace and Bobbie Lee. Miss Ruth and RM, who had a still up in the mountains whose recipe for mash was so clean, I was told, that the police in three counties would drive a hundred miles just to rinse their mouths with it.

Was real easy to tell when I was getting close. There were signposts. I'd pass the last of the rotted, bug infested billboards that were still standing, bound together, not by bailing wire and chewing gum, but by cathedrals of praying insects, weevils on their knees, they'd say, saved by the glorious Word, still trying with everything they had left to keep the sign vertical, their final redemption, asking you for the faith honey, just the faith. All sticky and sweet.

I'd pass the paint chipped windows anointed with the taped cut outs of Christ Jesus, facing out, or just around the corner, the promise of Boo Radley lurking behind Tennessee Williams at the next rest stop, drinking sweet iced tea mixed with hard Rye, with Horton Foote, Faulkner

87

and Beauchamp, dear Beauchamp, talking about the old times, dripping salt chaw over his cracked lips.

I'd look out the window and see the familiar warped sign that had survived the winter and announced "Turkee Shoot every Thursday at 6:00 PM," scrawled hastily on the scrapped flat of crooked plywood. From the road, at the right speed, the sign would lean towards you, nonchalantly, goading you to come on down, take your best shot. Dare ya sweetie.

Then there were the strip clubs set down right next to the Baptist churches with names like The Rabbit Hole and Buck Shot, where angelic, where cherubic, wore sequined G-strings that cut the flesh into fine innocent baby rolls and rounded them into soft protruding waves that curved and taunted while their babies cried in the corners, cradled by more spangled plumpness during a break, while Mom pumped her ass for the money.

These were dirt roads with a clear direction, with destinies, a familiarity of where to go and why, of signs stretching to the horizon for fresh corn, heirloom tomatoes and sweet peaches, homemade jams, pancake and waffle houses, hot biscuits, chicken gravy, grits with butter and fried chicken wallowing in tallow so thick that you could spoon it out, drop it on toast, spread it all around and then cover it with crab apple jelly.

When I would get to the crest of the hill to take a piss at the rest stop just above town, I knew that there would be a man in the bathroom, standing in the corner with a jar of glistening hair pomade, with little to do and nowhere else to go. He'd personally thank me for coming, pull a paper towel, hand it to me, say "thank you "sir," and back away slowly with his hands cupped, palm up, more of a supplication than an offer. On the chipped counter, you could choose between a Scope or Listerine, pre-poured in tiny white cups or you could pick from a plate of stale mints for a buck and perhaps consider using one of the combs that had been marinating in a mason jar of cobalt blue since last Easter, take it out, slow and easy, slide it through your hair, as if to say, "now I'm ready."

I'd swing by the convenience counter on my way out and buy some food that had been made in a back room six months ago, still settling on a buyer, waiting for someone to say, "sure, I'll give it a go." Pickled eggs or spiced pig's feet that I could buy from a woman so friendly that you knew that if you asked her, she'd drop everything and leave with you just so you would buy her some new shoes, slide them on for her, then let you slowly take them off while you licked your lips, so she could slink into your motel bed in black silk, dripping hot fat, sizzling on the sheets with her knees apart, her toes digging into the mattress.

Ended up getting the speeding ticket right before Tuberville. Pulled me over and told me the ticket was going to be $425, but if I wanted to hang around town for a few days and pay the fine in person next Wednesday, the judge would reduce the ticket to $100. Cop looked into the back seat and wanted to know if the stripper, the baby and the barefoot girl in the backseat were family. Told him they were just along for the ride but did mention that I was heading up to RM's sometime before dinner and would pick him up a bottle.

# Brian R. Martens

Brian has always been a poet. His first book *Three Raven Gate*, (2019) consists of Haiku and other favorite poems; his second manuscript is *Merlin's Wing*.

His podcast is *The Spoken Symbol*.

Brian has a Masters in Organization Development and offers workshops on Myth/Ancient Stories & Creativity to small businesses and organizations and is a California Poet In the Schools instructor.

Brian co-hosts the Santa Rosa Arts Center, "Speakeasy": santarosaartscenter.org/index.php/speakeasy.

www.brianrmartens.com

# The Rilke

*Brian R. Martens*

*Homage for Rilke's poem, The Panther*

Timid in hat and coat,
sitting on a bench
in the Paris Zoo,
he stares.

Sitting apart from comfort,
his body hidden,
barring him from an opening
to see into the animals.

He comes day after day
observing me, testing his will
to discover a path, to pierce
and expose inside.

Daily, imprisoned within hat and coat,
his vision paces less, moves further,
until he trusts.

Through time, his introspection
sees past his contentment,
begins to penetrate
inside my animal essence.

His eyes seize me,
without the believed bars
passing, knows the thread is felt
between us, and suddenly he's aware,

I am Panther.

# Dreaming in Trees

I'm walking to the river,
with my grandson
asleep in his stroller.
The tiny wheels a rhythm
of crunching leaves,
rolling gravel, smooth dirt,
twigs crumbling.

This sleepy rhythm—
walking, strolling,
wind, birds, breath,
in, out through his fluid chest—
keeps his dream alive.

The fertile unconscious
hears the Earth speak,
a walking meditation
mesmerizing this Buddha.

Not to wake him
from his appointed dream,
merging this nature with his nature,
I sit to watch the nomadic river.

Standing up, I again embark,
calmness his pillow,
as he sleeps silently.

As we stroll, he wakes, "Papa."
I stop, kneel to him.
Gushing out of his dream, he
looks up and points to the trees.

"Were you dreaming?" I ask,
"In the trees, in the trees, up, up, up,"
he delights.

In his eyes, I see the fervent passion of life
awaken. Through his thousand lips, I hear
God.

# Jackson's nose

*Brian R. Martens*

smells every green thing,
quivering nostrils,
each vibrates a different tune,
the left side classical,
right side Hip-Hop.

His body sways
to the blue road in between.
He doesn't mind
there's no sound in space.
The smells of chartreuse
enter his nose in octaves,
arpeggios, bumped by clef signs.

Birds add a riff,
black-brown root,
a gong of respect, humming.

He looks at wires in the sky
hears his voice repeated.
Space walking with Bach
worms watch from their squirming trail.

Cacophony laughing
at bent ears of wind
holding the symphony, instruments

of glee. Bee's, the back beat
of pollinating stories.

Jackson walks up to me, back-fires
his horn, laying down his track,
sprawling it over tuned keys,
notes of peaches, tuna,
and throaty meow.

Silence goes deep
below the high notes.
He is the bass, below bass,
the purple/black,
below music, below sound.

He flares both nostrils
making music.

# Blowtorch

*Brian R. Martens*

*"I think every woman should have a blowtorch."*
— Julia Child

Every female child educated
in the proper use of a blowlamp,
would lessen abuse in the world,
would bring more gender equality.

Girls and women, fitted with twin holsters,
a Bernzomatic for each hand,
in case one runs out of fuel.

There would be quick draw contests,
useful to thwart that touchy neighbor
or family member. A Red Dragon
used to singe an eyebrow
and prevent acts of aggression.

A boon for plastic surgeons,
repairs for grabby hands, hospital
burn units triple staffed, empowered
females snickering about the latest
torching incidents.

Julia was ahead of her time, envisioned
more uses than the harmless, Crème Brûlée.

Bosses and coworkers would risk getting
their ties singed, and explaining
to their partners.

Torches would be brought into
courtrooms igniting judge's robes
for not abiding a restraining order.

After maiming much of the population,
leaders would learn to work respectfully
with owners of a Spicy Dew Torch.

The use of the blowtorch would return
to more mundane uses—
starting the barbeque grill, lighting
candles for a special dinner,
and the occasional Crème Brûlée.

# Sarah Paris

Sarah is a Swiss-American poet, writer, photographer, editor, and former journalist.

She is the author of two novellas, *The Hermit*, and *The Traveler* (as Chris Solano); *Waywards*, a collection of short stories; and the German-language novel *Ahnenbeschwörung*, published in Switzerland. She is also a widely published haiku poet.

# The Sentry

*Sarah Paris*

## The Woman from Alturas

She tilted the water bottle to catch the last few drops. The warm breeze blowing in through the open window only made her hotter. Her air conditioner had broken down, as had the GPS, so she had taken a wrong turn at Cedarville and ended up on this unpaved road. She knew she needed to turn around but was still hoping to get back to a paved highway where she could reorient herself.

When she spotted the handmade sign, all that her eyes could see was the word "water." She hit the brakes, pulled over, and got out. The sign was leaning against a wooden shack. Next to it stood a rickety chair, and now she saw the man sitting there. His cowboy hat shaded a lined, brown face. Stringy grey hair fell down his back. But his tattooed arms were muscular. The woman stopped in her tracks.

"Hi …" she said, looking around nervously. There was no sign of another human — there hadn't been for the last couple of miles. Should she dash back into her car?

The man didn't look at her, just pointed his thumb to the open doorway. "Help yourself."

She could feel the sweat on her neck. Her tongue was stuck to the roof of her mouth. She had to have water!

When she stepped into the shack, it took her a moment to adjust to the dim light. There was one long, wooden table, and on it, two bronze containers with spouts. On each spout hung a sign. One said "water," the other "tea." Two rows of glasses were neatly lined up in between.

On the other end of the table were two baskets, one holding bundles of dried meat, strung together by raffia, the other containing similarly bundled, hand-rolled cigarettes.

"You don't have any … bottled water?" the woman asked, her voice creaky from dryness.

*Stupid question.* She knew she should just turn around and get out of there. Yet she kept staring at the bronze water tank with its sheen of condensation. Where had she seen one just like that? A memory flashed into her mind. The holy water dispenser at St. Brigid's, back when she was a girl. Her mother always sent her there with a bottle to fill for the font at home.

"Where does this water come from?"

"Quaking Asp Spring. Get it myself." The man nodded towards the tabletop mountain in the distance. "Don't worry, it's clean. The glasses too."

She held one up towards the light. It sparkled.

God, she was thirsty.

She filled the glass with water and checked it. It was clear and cold enough to cool her hands. How could it be this chilled, sitting on a table in a shack in the middle of the desert?

*Oh, what the hell. Better to die from poison than from thirst.* She gulped down the water. It was so delicious that her eyes welled up with tears. Quickly, she refilled the glass and drank again, then sighed with relief.

*Everything was going to be fine.*

The woman wasn't sure how long she'd been standing there, leaning against the table, every once in a while sipping more water. When she finally emerged from the shack, the sun appeared to be lower on the horizon.

"What do I owe you?" she asked. The man was smoking something in a pipe. It didn't smell like tobacco, nor like weed.

"It's paid for," the man said.

She looked at him in confusion, but he didn't say anything else, just gazed through the smoke into the distance. The woman hesitated.

"I think I'm lost. Which way is Winnemucca?"

Now the man turned to her and gave her a long look. His eyes were bright green in his brown face.

"I don't think you want to go there," he said.

And she knew he was right.

## *The Girl from Winnemucca*

The small cloud of dust on the horizon turned into a motorcycle that came tearing down the dirt road, slowing its speed just enough to come to a gravel-splashing stop in front of the shack. Its rider pulled off a dust-caked helmet, shook out a mop of blond hair, and looked around. Her eyes fell on the figure slouched in a chair in a strip of shade.

"Where the hell am I?" she called out in a husky voice. "Man, one minute I'm on a paved road in California, next I'm on a dirt road in the middle of fucking nowhere."

The girl — she looked to be no older than eighteen — got off her bike, all the while talking.

"I knew I'd taken a wrong turn at Cedarville. Hell, it's not like this motorcycle has GPS. And I lost my phone. Not that I expect there's any reception in this godforsaken place. But I have to get to Reno tonight! And I'm so fucking tired."

All ten of her fingers went into her hair in an effort to comb it away from her face.

"Did I mention I'm almost out of gas? Do you have gas?" She didn't wait for an answer. "No, of course not. Do you serve coffee at least? What's this sign say?" She glanced over at the handmade sign leaning against the shack's wall. "Tea. Does it have caffeine in it?"

The man tipped back his tattered cowboy hat to look at her then shook his head.

"Nope. Herb tea. Try the jerky."

She rolled her eyes.

"Jerk yourself," she muttered, got back on her bike and tried to kick it into action, but it only sputtered. She tried again. Same result.

"Fuck."

The girl looked around. Miles of brown desert and no signs of life except for this dismal shack and the skinny old guy sitting in front of it who clearly didn't give a damn about her troubles. Tea and jerky, what a joke. Was there even a bathroom? She got off her bike again and entered the shack to scope out what was there. Holy shit. Nothing but a rough wood table with two urns marked "water" and "tea" and two baskets. One held bundles of dried meat, the other one hand-rolled cigarettes.

"Seriously? You think you can sell this stuff?" she called to the guy outside.

"It's free."

"Yeah, it better be. What's this, squirrel meat?"

"Antelope jerky."

"Next thing you're going to tell me you hunted the antelope yourself."

"Yep."

The girl laughed. If she wasn't so desperate to get to Reno tonight, this would have been funny. *Maybe it will be funny. Once I make it. If I make it. Oh God, please, please …*

She closed her eyes, suddenly feeling faint, so that she had to reach out and hold on to the table to steady herself. *Okay, maybe I do need to eat something.* She took a closer look at the jerky. It looked normal. No worse that what you get at a gas station. She broke off a little bit, licked it, then chewed tentatively. Her mouth filled with flavor. Not just the taste of salt and spice and smoke-dried meat, but something else. What? She broke off another piece, popped it into her mouth, chewed. Hunger filled her like rage. She chewed and ate and drank some of the water, sat on the table, ate some more. At last, she felt full. Not just full. Rested. All her weariness had disappeared.

"Hey man, seriously, what do I owe you?" she said as she stepped out of the shack.

"It's on the house. The gas too."

"What gas?"

He just pointed to the bike. She checked the gas gauge. It was full.

"Where did that come from?"

He didn't answer, instead, he pointed west. "You need to get yourself back to Cedarville and don't try to take the south road. Take the 395 instead. You'll be in Reno before dark."

*And she will make it.*

The girl's eyes popped open. The words had appeared in her mind out of nowhere. Had he said them? She glared at the man, but he was already slumped back in his chair, the cowboy hat tilted over his eyes. The girl shrugged, got on her bike, started it. The engine sprang into life with a satisfying rumble. She turned around and headed west, not even wondering why the sun was still so high in the sky when she had arrived in the late afternoon.

## Two Boys from Cedarville

A mud-covered Chevy truck rolled up in front of the shack, and two boys embarked with a swagger and with grins trying to be sneers.

"Well, how about that," the taller one drawled, "looks like our buddy was right — there's some kind of store here. And just one old guy minding it."

The figure who was sitting on a chair in the shade glanced at them from underneath his weather-beaten cowboy hat. The two boys scanned the dirt road that seemed to stretch forever into the emptiness of the Nevada desert. Then the taller one spoke again:

"Dude, got any beer?"

The man's lined, brown face showed no expression except for the keen gaze in his bright green eyes.

"Nope."

"No? Whatcha got then?"

The taller boy walked into the shack and looked around.

"'ll be damned! Man, you gotta come and look at this shit."

The shorter boy followed him inside where he stopped, his face puzzled.

"I don't get it. What is this?"

A rough table held two copper urns with spouts on which hung signs reading "tea" and "water." Next to them, two baskets held bundles of what appeared to be dried meat in one and hand-rolled cigarettes in the other.

"Dude! There was supposed to be a store here!" the taller boy exclaimed. "Buddy said it was a store. This is just crap!" He tried to lift the table as if to overturn it, but the wood was heavy and didn't budge. He walked out, followed by his sidekick.

"Old man, this isn't cool. We came here to grab some brewskis."

"Sorry to disappoint," the man murmured.

"Yeah, you should be sorry alright." The boy looked around and saw a trailer perched on the hill above the shack, next to some trees. His eyes narrowed.

"You live here by yourself?"

"Yep."

"You some fugitive from your tribe or something? Had to get out of the rez?"

"If you say so."

"Old injun, all alone, ain't you worried someone's gonna rob you?"

"Of what?"

"Oh, I don't know." The boy scratched the light stubble on his chin and looked back at the trailer. "Bet you got some cash stashed away up there."

"You'd be wrong."

"You sure?"

With a grin, the boy pulled a gun from his jeans jacket. He gestured to his friend.

"Joey, why don't you go up there and take a look."

Joey, whose black hair was slicked down with gel and who couldn't have been more than fifteen, looked dubious.

"I don't know, Buck. Maybe it's locked."

"Is it locked, dude?"

Buck waved his gun in front of the man who didn't react.

"Nope."

"Exactly! So what are you waiting for, Joey?"

The younger boy started to walk up the hillside. The terrain was rough, and he had to circle around a group of boulders. When he was halfway up to the top where the trailer stood, his left leg suddenly dropped away, and he let out a sharp yelp of pain.

"What? What happened?" Buck shouted.

"I got hurt!" Joey yelled.

"Oh, you damn fool!" Buck placed the gun closer to the old man's face. "Now listen, old man: You stay right here and don't move, got it?"

The man didn't move, except for a twitch at the right corner of his mouth, but the boy was already scrambling up the hill after his friend.

"Bonehead, why can't you ever watch where you're going," he hollered. Reaching his younger friend, he checked his ankle. "That's just a sprain, come on." He helped him down the hillside, half supporting his limp, half carrying him. When they had arrived back at the shack, he handed him the gun, then ordered the old man: "Get up and let my friend sit down!"

The man obligingly stood up, and Joey gingerly lowered himself onto the rickety chair. Buck handed him the gun.

"Now you watch him, and I'll go up."

Joey pointed the gun at the old man, but his hand was shaking.

"Be careful," the man said, "you don't want that to go off by accident."

He was now openly grinning. Joey glanced over to where Buck was making his way up the hillside. He saw him almost reaching the trailer, when something reared up in the brush. Now it was Buck's turn to yell, and his yell was louder than Joey's had been. He stumbled backwards, and something else raised itself up not three feet away from him with a loud rattle. The boy jumped as if hit by a cattle prod, then sprinted downhill at lightning speed.

"Holy shit!" he screamed, arriving back at the shack, breathing hard. "That hill is lousy with rattlers! How can you live in a place like this? You crazy?"

"It suits me," said the old man. He went inside the shack and came out with two glasses filled with a golden liquid.

"Here. Have some tea. It will steady your nerves."

Buck reeled back.

"You think you can poison us with that stuff?"

But Joey took the offered glass and sniffed it.

"Smells like peppermint tea. I'm thirsty!" He emptied the glass, then smiled with a deep sigh. "That tasted real good."

His friend watched him as if expecting him to go into convulsions. But Joey kept smiling as if something blissful had occurred to him. Buck took a tiny sip, then a larger one. He shook his head as if to say, hell no, I won't do this. Yet, as if overcome by a thirst greater than his will, he gulped down the liquid. Then he stared into the distance for some long minutes.

The old man walked up to him and took the gun.

"Now go back to Cedarville and tell your friend he was mistaken. There's nothing here but ghosts."

## The Man from Vya

It was late afternoon, and storm clouds were brewing in the west, when a car approached the shack. It did not appear to be in a hurry and so took a while before it became discernible as an old Jeep, covered with desert dust. With a squeal of rusty brakes, it stopped in front. The man who got out wore khaki pants, a hunter's vest, and his bare arms and broad face had seen a great deal of sun. He grinned, revealing a gap in his front teeth.

"Howdy!"

The old man who sat in front of the shack responded with a grunt. His visitor scanned the dilapidated building with its saggy beams.

"I just came from Vya. The ghost town, you know?"

The old man gave a slight nod.

"I'm obsessed with ghost towns," the visitor declared. "Or perhaps with ghosts." He squinted his eyes to better see the trailer that was sitting on the hill behind the shack. "You must have seen a few yourself, living out here."

"Could be."

Undeterred, the visitor smiled and pointed to the shack's entrance. "Mind if I have a look inside?"

"Help yourself."

The one room was dimly lit by a single bulb hanging from the rafters. The visitor carefully examined the items spread out on a rough table — two urns; one with water, one with tea; two baskets; one with jerky, the other with bundles of hand-rolled cigarettes.

"Do you sell these things?" he called to the old man outside.

"They're free."

"Got it."

The man lifted a bundle of cigarettes and sniffed.

"Weed?"

"Nope. Local herbs."

The man sniffed again, then pulled one out, stuck it in between his lips and lit it with a vintage silver lighter. He took a careful drag and blew out the smoke.

"Reminds me of those herbal cigarettes we used to puff on when I was a kid. Drove our parents crazy. Hey, have you got a bathroom around here by any chance?"

"There's an outhouse in the back."

The man walked around the shack and discovered a small hut a short distance behind the building, half hidden between two large boulders. It turned out to be relatively clean, as rural outhouses go. After he had finished his business and reemerged, he turned around to take another look at the boulders.

*Interesting. A bit like two trolls, bending towards each other*, he thought.

His cigarette had gone out, and he relit it and smoked it to the end, still looking around at the hillside, the sage brush, and the sky that had turned a deeper blue.

*God, I love the desert!* he thought. *Being away from all the craziness. Space to think, to relax. I could stay here forever.*

A gust of wind lifted his thin, long hair. He needed another hat. His last one was in a ditch somewhere.

With a sigh, he returned to the front of the shack. The old man had disappeared. So had the Jeep. There was only the rickety chair, and on it, the old man's weather-beaten cowboy hat.

The man stared at the chair for a while. Then he grinned, put on the hat, and sat down.

An hour later, a car drove up, and a woman stepped out. She looked around hesitantly.

"Hi ..." she said, apparently wondering if she should dash back into her car. Her tongue flicked over her dry lips.

The man glanced at her from underneath this hat, the eyes in his brown face flashing bright green in the sun. He pointed with his thumb to the open doorway.

"There's water inside. Help yourself."

# High & Coo

*Sarah Paris*

first light
in my cup
a new moon

morning dew
caught in the spider web
a feather

summer heat
the drowsy dance of
hover flies

rainy day
the cat watches birds
online

harvest moon
on the wire
a string of crows

November sunset
the last hummingbird
gulps it down

*Mood Indigo*
great horned owls'
call and response

# Linda Loveland Reid

Linda is an author of two novels available on Amazon, and a Jack London Awardee. Her essays, poems, and prose appear in over 30 publications.

Linda teaches art history for Sonoma State University (SSU) and Dominican University in the Osher Lifelong Learning program. She earned two BAs from SSU, graduating *cum laude* in History and Art History.

Linda is a figurative and abstract painter, has directed community theater for 30 years, and serves on multiple boards of directors, and is the current president of Artist Workshop of Sonoma County.

Email: lindalreid100@gmail.com
Website: LindaLovelandReid.com

# Prologue from Novel: *Touch of Magenta*

*Linda L. Reid*

*Touch of Magenta* follows two women: Corri, who in 1971 grapples to decipher her past, and Pegeen, whose life unfolds beginning in 1895, revealing mysteries and hidden entanglements of three generations. Set in California Gold Country, San Francisco, Chinatown, Singapore, Italy and England, this story touches the universal need each of us has to know our own history. Integrity is not a simple thing.

## Sonora, California — 1899

A lantern sits on the landing atop the outdoor stairs, its dim light offering little solace to the grief within its reach. Tears blur Pegeen's vision and she can barely see to pull the strips of incense from their paper jacket. She stops at the sound of a horse carriage, listens. Her heart racing, on her knees and with trembling fingers, she lights each incense stick, then fastens the wooden end into the dirt on top of the grave. She struggles to her feet, stands still for a moment, then, slowly makes three traditional bows. Sitting down beside the dark mound, she hugs a shawl round her shoulders and watches as the incense smoke rises, giving off a sweet, pungent smell. She waits until the last sliver wafts upward.

## *Sonora, California — 1971*

Disallowing what she believes to be a barbaric custom of throwing a handful of dirt onto the coffin, Corri picks a pansy from the pot and gently tosses it down into the gaping hole. It floats, catches a breeze and whirls round, the purple petals rippling like a feather, until it drops in slow motion down, gently settling on top of the coffin. A soft breath of loss whispers from her lips, "Goodbye." She kneels down, careful not to rest her stockinged knee on the muddy ground. What words? How to say what cannot be said? A pair of men's shoes come into view at the edge of the gravesite. "Are you all right?" the voice says, "May I help?" "What?" she responds, disoriented. Then, in an instant, a wild rush of adrenalin shoots through her body. She looks up, unbelieving. This person—out of context—she opens her mouth to speak, but no words form.

# Excerpt from: *Something in Stone*

*Linda L. Reid*

## *1977 Healdsburg*

The Aven movie theater used to be their den of iniquity, a dark haven for young lovers. Chris smiled to think of the rows of teenagers clutched close and the usher pacing up and down the aisle, looking for bad stuff.

Two movies burned in Chris's erotic education, both screaming something about her body. In "Peyton Place," Lana Turner lived in an innocent town like Healdsburg. Everyone was doing something scandalous, mostly with their neighbors. But it was "The Outlaw," starring Jane Russell, a big-breasted brunette discovered by crazy Howard Hughes that tapped a place inside, low down in her tummy, even lower. When that cowboy tore through that barn window and jumped on Jane, wrestling her around in the hay until Jane gave way to his kisses, well, something happened to Chris. It scared her, in an exciting way.

It was odd how landmarks become such a part of your life, Chris thought. Certainly the Aven figured in every stage of her maturity, what might be called navigation as a person desperately tries to figure out childhood to adulthood, and beyond.

The *beyond* part came to Chris when Brian died. One day she was an adult, a mom and wife, the next day she didn't know who she was. Her assistant, Marta, kept things going, pretending to clients that Chris was in the office.

And, Marta left her alone to heal, until one day.

"Want to go to the movies?" Marta asked, a red tussle of curls flopping across her happy Irish face.

Marta and Chris went to see "King Kong," the remake of the 1930s classic with Fay Wray. Jessica Lange just didn't quite have the same vibe as Fay, but the story was the same: big strong animal after helpless girl. Halfway through, after sharing an obscenely large box of popcorn, just as King Kong had escaped and was wreaking havoc over New York, Marta reached over to Chris's lap and found her hand. Chris didn't move. Marta slowly began to caress Chris's hand, then slipped between Chris's legs and up her skirt. Before reaching its destination, Chris moaned and her head rolled back onto the seat. Later that night, Chris learned what she might have always suspected. There was nothing wrong with her libido.

"What happened to that cute assistant you had?" Rennie asked.

"She's around," Chris replied.

But Rennie knew. As Marta and Chris left the movie that night, before the good guys gunned King Kong down from the Empire State Building, Chris saw Rennie's head whip around.

Only a week lapsed before Rennie was on the phone to Chris. "Let's have lunch."

They met at The Healdsburg House, the only real restaurant in town.

Before that the choices narrowed to Lonnie's hamburger joint and a cafe called The Tip Top at the north end of town that offered live music on Friday nights—well, a guitar player and sometimes a guy on the accordion. The Healdsburg House was a smash success from day one with crowds waiting to get in. Phone calls jammed the lines. "Let's have lunch!" Meaning cocktails and fancy-dressed waiters, right in town.)

After a drink, they all relaxed a bit.

"Chris," Rennie began, "we have been close friends for years."

"Many, many years," Chris said, popping a cherry into her mouth, deftly wrung from her Manhattan.

"We should not have important things standing between us." Rennie smiled.

Abby didn't say a word, but did look at Chris as if to say "sorry."

Rennie continued. "It's been a year since Brian's death and I know how difficult it has been."

"Do you?" Chris replied.

"I saw you with your assistant in the show, and well, Chris, if you are gay, then say so."

"I'm gay."

"Oh, my God!" Rennie gasped.

Abby's eyes opened wide.

"We care," Rennie managed.

"And so do I," Chris said. "Look, this has been a huge shift for me. At first it was fun. Then, the next day, I got plenty scared. I have a son, a granddaughter, and a business. <u>And</u>," she reached over to squeeze Rennie's hand, "<u>friends</u>. Why would I want to all of a sudden turn lesbian?"

Rennie and Abby stared, waited.

"But here's what I learned. You don't 'turn' lesbian. You just are. I'm happy. Even with all of the trouble this will bring, I feel like I'm finally in my own skin."

"We love you," Rennie said.

Abby dabbed at her eyes.

"Let's not be sad for heaven's sake." Chris smiled. "I'm celebrating. And, by the way, thank you for caring." Chris set her glass down. "And I do mean thanks. We're family, lucky to have each other, <u>trying as it often is</u>. I'm okay. Better than okay. Do you know, sex has never been exciting for me? Now it is."

"Oh, my God," Rennie said.

Abby fiddled with her fork. "If it's the right thing for you, Chris, we support you."

Rennie looked around at the other tables. (draw out) "It's not fashionable."

"What?" Chris smiled. "Sex? I've often wondered."

"Don't be funny," Rennie frowned. "I know this is California, modern, big deal 1977, *but still.*"

"I'll be smart," Chris winked.

"People get careless," Rennie warned. "People like…"

"Lesbians?" Chris interjected.

"All I'm saying," Rennie whispered, "is that we should all be careful."

"Don't tell me, Rennie," Chris whispered back. "You too—a lesbian?"

"You're a scream," Rennie snapped.

They enjoyed another round of drinks and Chris especially loved her big plate of beef Stroganoff. She was indeed hungry. Like a wild stallion.

# Abstract

*Linda L. Reid*

I labor love onto that space
What does this painting want to be

Want of me
What color is Tuesday
Black is the soul — yellow, the music
Smear freedom — deep maroon and bone of mind
Swirls of ruby red
 I witness my own stammer
Irrepressible unheard music vibrates the canvas
Color is a thumbprint of emotion
Meaning plunges to the bottom, rolls around
I breath in paint
Accept the mark — be Zen with this wild thing
Emerge into the line, devour the next splash of idea

Surge myself to the attack
What appears when I think of joy
It's about courage — spend four hours…fail…go again
Splatter energy
When was the last time you did something for the first
    time
Rout virgin white — a palette knife, color dripping with
    intent
Sweeping curve of cerulean sets a circle
An arc of desire

Some paintings, touched by greatness, will never be just *a painting*,
Searing me into the moment. A moment
when that gold is Autumn, quietly whispering,
*I'm here*
What do I do with these feelings
No feeling is the last.
Magic is the color of magenta and it comes from
Saying "yes"

# Vortex of Me

*Linda L. Reid*

I'll never know what it's like to be an angel, says Gabriel
delivering the news to Mary,
To see her expression, of what — delight? Anxiety?
We are in the realm
of miracles.
Angels are cherubs or are they fairies?
I have a friend, a robust poet/artist of a man
who captured fairies in Ireland in a beautiful small box.
Bought them home to Sebastopol.
Really.
How wonderful.
I will not go down into a vortex, that blue-deep space
where my spirit guide might dwell. My sister's guide is a
 bear.
A friend has six vortexes in her backyard.
There are shamans and drumming.
Another dimension.
Maybe.
Am I so utterly filled that there is no need to go beyond,
to let in more life?
A heart sated with family, husbands, art.
Do I not already hunt down the next challenge?
Is that enough
to prove worthiness?
Are others more *woke* — my sister more in-tune?
They call it *speciation*, that moment of crossing the

evolutionary threshold.
Finding the human spectrum that is latent
(they say),
inside us.
I'm not likely to step to the right of my left-brain
    hemisphere.
Not once have I allowed my fortune to be told,
my life pronounced by another.
I mean, what does 'more life' look like?
More stuff — more commitments?
More joy.
I'll never be many things.
 But I've come to grips with
the cacophony that makes up me.
For better or worse,
I am my own spirit.
That other door is closed.
And yet —

# Sunday Dinners

*Linda L. Reid*

I don't know how to get back to Sunday dinners
Canning peaches, making applesauce
We kids used to grouse at a perfectly good
afternoon trapped at grandma's.
Her house was hot, but she did have that big trunk
full of odd and fascinating things,
like her long braid, wacked off
and kept all those years.
Do BBQs solve the problem, family milling about,
beer and coke on the back lawn?
I think the word is yearn,
or maybe nostalgia.
Is it more family I'm missing?
Is it that everyone has grown up, moved on?
"I'm just a relic," a friend cried to me.
I tell her, take what you can get.
They love you but we are
 not the wheelhouse anymore.
*Rage, rage against the dying of the light.*
I still color my hair golden.

# Seconds

*Linda L. Reid*

Heart, breath, blood.
We are only those few seconds from not existing.
Every living thing is a survivor,
a whisp, an illusion until the next minute.
God is subtle, Einstein said, but not malicious.
Outstretched, we grab blindly at the hem of humanity.
We sense the urgency of oxygen, the danger of carbon
    monoxide.
We shudder with the bird who finds his feeder empty.
The insouciant step hides our fear.
We innately feel, like the man returning to the battlefield
    where he lost his leg.
Like a woman returning to the place where he loosened
    her hair.
Love wants to recapture the smile that started it all.
We take strange solace from Dionysus,
from his passion and especially from his downfall.
Life is fleeting, someone famously said, never lasting.
We must die, some think, to live forever.
Are we dust to dust as we attempt to swallow whole this
    one life?
Is it one life or many? No matter.
And yet, I am without a God — humanity is my oracle.
I break into a million atoms
What of today?
Seconds are what we live on.

# Gabriela Vannier

Gabriela's work has appeared in several publications. She draws inspiration from authors such as Jeannette Walls and Mary Karr, appreciating their candid and vulnerable storytelling. Ms. Vannier is currently working on a memoir and a collection of poetry and short stories.

# before the tiger rain

*Gabriela Vannier*

sickly saffron sky
provoke ominous rainclouds
burst forth, crimson pall

# When I Was Alive

*Gabriela Vannier*

When I was alive the sun rose and set on me, for me
My father's twinkling eyes told me so

When I was alive my touch could heal a neighborhood cat
My proof, my mother's pride

When I was alive I moved effortlessly here, there
Via saddle shoes or tires or skates
The wind in my hair gave me flight

When I was alive I quenched my thirst on bright red fruit
As its sugary juice ran over my knees and into the gutter
With the black and shiny cast-offs

When I was alive
I caused no pain, had no regrets

When I was alive I had no idea
How soon my death would come

# as

*Gabriela Vannier*

as

the Bramble Cay Melomys of the Australian Great Barrier
   Reef
and Persia, Prussia, Austria and the West Pier

as

the Nasturtium eating Madeiran White Butterfly
and the Baiji, "Goddess of the Yangtze" River

as

the Golden Toad of the elfin cloud forest
and Amelia, Diana and Sylvia P

as

the Old Man of the Mountain,
the memoir of Lord Byron
a burned out star
melted snow

She is
so

# apricot

*Gabriela Vannier*

once I was gangly and shapeless in boys underwear
clinging to the branch of an apricot tree reaching for the
    sweet plump fruit
now I am here and joy is in the stone at the center of the
    sticky fruit that hangs
beyond my grasp

sadness is the once sturdy tree now fragile with seasons
it's wilted leaves and brittle branches reflected in the glass
quietness comes as the sun's last ray dips below the horizon
    turning everything
to black

soon I will be lost in dreams and I shall climb the tree
and I will pluck the tender fruit and cradle it in both hands
before I devour it

# midnight

*Gabriela Vannier*

at waters edge I've scoured the earth
*Where have you gone my love?*

twas sweet
the moment we shared on the drifts of whitecaps and
    slumber
buried too deep to be seen

and now before me the infinite blue
            I lift my eyes to the deep horizon
            where midnight meets midnight

the piercing pale of your eyes
your cool soft and tender hands studying my body like
    braille
    the classic sculpted piece I once had memorized
                        now slowly slipping away

# Seven Fingers

*Gabriela Vannier*

To paint like Chagall, seven fingers you'd need
Surely five would not suffice
With seven fingers, imagine the speed

At which your creative desires are freed
At sale, just think the asking price
To paint like Chagall, seven fingers you'd need

To paint like Chagall, seven fingers you'd need
For choosing the colors, dark to light
And putting on canvas the image you dreamed

Oh what a curiosity to see
The creation of Joseph and Potiphar's Wife
To paint like Chagall, seven fingers you'd need

His library of works are as vast as the sea
The brides and the bovidae, his artistic device
To paint like Chagall, seven fingers you'd need

To paint like Chagall, seven fingers you'd need
To paint like yourself would five fingers suffice?
Notwithstanding the digits, inspiration takes lead
And when you behold it, will your art provoke glee?

# o heavy soul

*Gabriela Vannier*

o heavy soul
your burden like darkness betrays me
of wisp and of woe
two lovers entwined in a dance
with fear and with fury
the hours like minutes erase me
o heavy soul
oh won't you release me at last?

# birdsong night

take flight
you light-footed phantom
regret not the passage of the hours
whilst your gossamer head lay secrets beneath my pillow
twisting in the linen
and haunting other places vanishing from view

peering through the window dampened by my breath
I watch the curling coils of rainfall hideaway
through grates and underfoot
choking unseen places

oh veiled intruder
you are out there

still
the rain is falling
blowing about in the wind
and I shall wait by the window
for you to come again

# Judith Vaughn

Judith Vaughn lives in Sonoma, California, with Tim, her husband, and Louie, their Catahoula puppy.

She is a member of PoeticLicenseSonoma; California Writers Club, Redwood Writers branch; and Sebastopol Center for the Arts Poetry Salon.

Her poetry has been published in several anthologies, '21-'25. The most recent: *Kinds of Cool, A Collection of Jazz Poetry;* Joe Maita, Editor, '25; and *Reverberations 3 — A Visual Conversation;* SebastopolCenter for the Arts, '24, as well as in literary reviews online.

# A Red Fox

*Judith Vaughan*

On the hills above the valley, trees cast shadows
on yellow drenched hills of diminishing summer.
Grounded no more in roots of old trees, shadows
pirouette onto the hillside stage.

In wind, silhouettes whirl across golden strands of grass.
In late afternoon sun, not quite moon, they preen for eyes
of red tailed hawks, black ravens, red-headed vultures
    overhead.

Night darkness slowly enfolds the hills, fills the valley;
shadows reluctantly return to the old trees. Below them,
stone walls stacked along the highway sit silent.
A red fox glances at the moon.

# Ode to Gerald Stern and Freddie Mercury

*Judith Vaughan*

Freddie Mercury wrote a song about Galileo,
a far cry from Gerald Stern's poetic musing
on a squirrel seeking life's meaning on a green
and wild hillside just across the road.

A road filled with speeding trucks, impatient
drivers, no attention paid to the quivering fandango
dancer waiting for a moment's relief from its terror,
a quick passage to the other side.

Freddie killed a man, no four-legged critter, yellow
teeth ground down to dust. Freddie, the squirrel
in another life, body aching, shivers up and down
his spine. No wild hillside in his future.

No one longs for death, thunderbolt and lightning,
speeding trucks or guns to forehead. Nothing really
matters anyway the wind blows, nothing really matters.
We are just a piece of paper blowing in the wind.

# First Chair

*Judith Vaughan*

I don't recall if my mother ever gazed at me
as if I were the first sunrise seen from earth.
If she did it was before memory.

I do recall sitting in the comfort of her lap
on a couch that had seen better days. Her voice
a salve on the pained heart of her grown daughter.

Her gaze not a sunrise, but her words music to me
"if you weren't my daughter I would like you anyway."
The smile on her face a cello singing first chair.

# September 23, 1926 — John Coltrane's Birthday

*Judith Vaughan*

I want to talk about John Coltrane, how dead stars fell to
    earth,
cosmic dust revived as music formed in a placenta,
    developed
in a mother's womb. Not just any womb, that of Alice
    Blair Coltrane,
the mothership of genius.

The moment he came from between her legs, screamed
    out his birth
cry, Gaia paused her sun trajectory, blessed him with a
    welcoming
tune he carried for all his days and nights. He gathered
    his star dust
into form, joined blue owls in flight, a mystical experience.

He joined other incandescents, Bird, Miles, Monk. They
    flew with
blue owls on the backs of pentatonic scales, entered the
    realm
of gods. Mortals listened, eyes closed, transported to a
    private
land lost to them in real time.

Then he died; Cosmic dust carried him back to empyrean
  sky,
a young star shining light and music.

# Gary Weiner

Gary Weiner has been writing, playing, singing and recording music since fourth grade. He recorded *Released at Last*, a full-length album with the aid of master musicians including Nina Gerber for his 70th birthday. The album release was held at the Sebastopol Center for the Arts to a sold-out crowd. He's also been showing his photography at galleries in San Francisco and at the old Sebastopol Center for the Arts building at what's now the Barlow.

www.garyweinerarts.com

# Rough and Ragged Road

*Gary Weiner*

### 1

On this rough and
ragged road,
littered with the downings and detritus of winter storms,
The twisted limbs, the shattered stone
All, rent by wrenching rain.

### 2

We awaken as
we are about to fall.
To fall down and down
to our soaked and shivering selves

### 3

Yet, we turn
We turn to our calloused and corn flecked feet
as they do their best
to do our will
And as we do our best to do theirs.

### 4

But that great horned owl —
just up there —
in the cragged, crooked oak,
(That elder who will fall one day as well,)

The great horned owl
hoots two times.

5

Ah!
Just so.
We *remember* again.
We remember again.
We remember we are *walking*.
We remember we are *only walking*.
We are walking on this
This very rough and ragged road.

6

Our time and our attention are bounded.
Our time and our attention will end.

Our time and our attention will end.

And yes, that great old, grizzled owl,
those round eyes
locked upon us —
those black-rimmed,
round and vibrant,
living whizzing bullet eyes,
those eyes lock upon our dark hat,
they lock upon our heavy coat.

Her eyes pierced our tramping oblivion.

## 7

Only now do our feet know each
rock and rivulet.
As do the muscles, the cords and discs,
All racked and rickety,
That keep our bending back,
Up,
right against this daunting hill
All on each rock and rivulet.

## 8

The air is cold.
The air, the very hand of Earth,
The air is on our face
On the face of our single, precious life.
The hand of Earth — always there-
the hand of Earth — compassion and love!
Yea, the hand of Earth holds us in her loving grace

## 9

She pilots us back on down the road
to the tattered,
flattened and threadbare
worn black cushion:

To sit and breathe.
To sit and breathe.
To sit and breathe.
To sit and breathe.
Amen.

# In Jaipur I Dream of Merri

*Gary Weiner*

In Jaipur,
In my damp bed,
In my sweaty head
I dream of Merri Weisbrot

Oh, how much I thought I loved her.

    Hindu Hindu Muslim Jain
    Muslim Hindu
    Hindu Jain

We walked home from school
To highland to rosewood
Past maple and elm
Then into the house of Morris and Lila

    Mad Mother Lila!
    No lights on Shabbos
    one Day of Rest
    Of rest from all
    Deep wells of worry

      B'rich hu!

One small failure
One grain of salt too few
Once through the door posts without blessing

Oh, bucket of flood!
Great, searing tragedy.
No good fortune no more hope.

Oh, poor Lila
What bad, bad wind blew so hard and
from where?

Come light the bright candles
Burn sweet cedar and clove
Rest in the night with Morris, your man.

In Jaipur, I dream of your daughter, sweet Merri

Hindu Hindu Muslim Jain
Muslim Hindu
Hindu Jain

"Disgraceful daughter!"
Say Morris and you
Lover of Tony Addalia
She runs from her tribe
For all of life's worth
Rending the tent of her father

Oh, poor porous tent!
Morris pulls out his pegs
And hurls them away
Far up to the sun
To vaporize in the furnace like they were nothing at all

But Merri, oh Merri
She runs round the world!
Her shoes are from China
Her shorts from Nogales
Her perfume is roses and sandalwood
She bathes in cardamom, nutmeg and saffron.

She shoulders reed baskets and
Sows seeds and wells
And bathtubs and butter
And long hoes and swabs
Making life better
For Hmong and Masai
And tiger and tapir and tree

>Hindu Hindu Muslim Jain
>Muslim Hindu
>Hindu Jain

Spirit Merri, with me in Jaipur
in hot sheets and gin.

White breasts adorned
With green feathers and figs.
Her thighs shine like marble
and mango and ghee
Gold bells in her hair and silver and copper and pearl
She dances in silks and with small cymbals.

>Hindu Hindu Muslim Jain
>Muslim Hindu
>Hindu Jain

Now slowing, she lowers
To Kashmiri silk carpet
On black agate bed
We hush and inhale

I'm Akbar I'm Sultan
I'm virile and bronze
I'm Mughal and Raj
my palace is pulsing

I leap up on her!
I leap then I suckle and stroke her fine breast

>              Hindu Hindu Muslim Jain
>              Muslim Hindu
>              Hindu Jain

Listen!
Long horns are blown.
Stiff mallets of jack wood
with tight heads of skin
Elephant drums in malarial frenzy

I am Ecstatic,
But I am alone,
And I'm done.

>              Hindu Hindu Muslim Jain
>              Muslim Hindu
>              Hindu Jain

Muslim Muslim Hindu Jain
Jain Jain
Hindu Jain

In Jaipur I dreamt of Merri
But left her behind in that room

See here is the street:

All Hindu and Muslim
And murder and flame.
All musk ox and dog,
All camel and soot
All hatred and anger
And crankshaft and shit
All black eyes and red teeth
All scratching at windows with raw, seething
wounds.

Raw, seething wounds!

Sing street mother.
Oh, Sing!

Hindu Hindu Muslim Jain
Muslim Hindu
Hindu Jain

Sing!

Muslim Muslim Hindu Jain
Jain Jain
Hindu Jain

Raw wounds!
And black flies!
One threadbare kurta
And a suggestion of shoe
All liquids and solids
Dull olive and brown

And babies on sidewalks
And rust jagged junk.

   Limp babies.
   Limp babies.
   Limp babies.

   Hindu Jain
   Hindu Jain
   Muslim Muslim
   Hindu Jain

What home is this?
What manner of hearth?

There in the dung the little girls twirl
In saris and sandals of orange and green
Bright colorful scarves of cotton and silk

I stumble and lurch dystrophic
Take refuge In Buddha.

These are yours, Tathagata, not mine

Send them home, Lord Buddha,
Send them home.

Set them to spinning and weaving
And cutting the place for our tombs

Cool caverns and columns
Revealed from the rock

      Right labor
      Right thought and
      Right heart

I hear no answering footsteps
No strike of a clapper on bowl
No shuffle of sandal on cobbles or trail
I hear no answering chant

      Muslim Muslim Hindu Jain
      Jain Jain Hindu Jain

Oh, dear Merri.
I've set you free.
Go dance for and run to the suffering ones.
Dance lentils and shelter.
Dance rice and dance peas.
And water. Just water.
Dance pure clear water
For them and for me.

# Period of Repose

A dispersed system —
a suspension,
an emulsion —
all agitated and opaque
needs time to settle.

First, the deluge.
The atmosphere burst open.
But overwhelmed rivers will recede.
Leaving hollows on soggy banks
That ground cannot yet hold me

When, though, the world gives back the sun,
After a period of repose,
the grains and flecks,
the countless specks
have mostly settled at last.

This ground,
Now, just dry enough,
Will hold me.

Across, on the other bank,
Across that endless always river,
I will sit on the other side.

# Kim Winter

Kim earned her MFA at the University of California, Santa Barbara and a BA in Art at Humboldt State University, Arcata, Ca. She also attended the Skowhegan School of Painting and Sculpture in Maine. Kim is an artist and has won several awards and is a member of the Sebastopol Center For The Arts Visual Art Team. Kim uses poetry in her art, adding words to enhance the meaning. In 2024, her ekphrastic poetry was published in the catalog for the Reverberations Art Exhibit.

360turnpike@gmail.com
Kimwinterartist.com
Instagram: winterart56

# I Get It

Kim Winter

The time went Daylight Savings.
I think I get it.
It's in my time frame.
So, yeah.
We are eating together today.
What is your silence?
Can I have a piece after lunch?
You reel me in. No. You real me in.
Actually you aren't even here.
You are in London. I am watering your plants.
There's a turkey on your patio peeking in every window.
"She's not here turkey."
We Belong Together plays on the radio — Ricki Lee
    Jones.
Re-incarnation?
Why not?

155

# Thinking on My Notepad

*Kim Winter*

Last night my dreams collided
with people I know,
people I don't know,
people I want to know.

I cry for my limping old dog.
I cry for that crow
who hit my windshield.
I cry for that little red squirrel
on the road.
I cry for that opossum,
furry pile of no-more life.
Opossums eat ticks.
I celebrate him.

As time lights my morning
I want to push it along
because that coyote out there,
in the dark,
wants to eat my cat.

I became the day
when I stepped into this morning.
I am trying to type something about myself.
I'm trying to remember things you were going to say.
If I was a fish I would be a flounder
because that's what I do.

Thinking on my notepad —
why can't I get this coffee
strong enough this morning.

# A Few Days Ago and Today

*Kim Winter*

Cruising car radio stations.
Maybe stop on a little Jesus talk
to wash our faces in some "good" words.
As I hear of the Gaza storm,
I see a load of Mclareons, Lamborginis,
and Peugeots on a truck sailing down Hwy 5.
Cows wallow in their muddy wishes of
green grass. Their corn fed guts growling.
Wrong for these cows.
Wrong of the government bad guys.
Yeah, lots of them.
They are snakes in the grass.
They eat pills to get rich, to get sex.
Today I want to be someone else.
I think I will have a martini
instead of a beer.

# Time

*Kim Winter*

Time is pinching me in the ass.
No,
It's grabbing me by the ass.
I swear it's turning my clock ahead when I
am not looking.
I don't have time to sleep.
I don't have time to stay awake.
I speak with commas so my thoughts
will never end.
More coffee please,
today with a donut.

# Morning Words

*Kim Winter*

The morning comes in the shape of a song
I can't get off my mind.
I want some words to put here
before the sun rises.
Yesterday I talked too much and burned
my mouth on the sky —
it was a beginning that never ended.
Crossing my fingers now
I watch the details of today.
If no one notices, I've got a secret.
You say my free thought
will land somewhere.
Eventually.

www.ingramcontent.com/pod-product-compliance
Lightning Source LLC
Chambersburg PA
CBHW070034260626
47159CB00005B/2033